PUFFIN BOOKS

*SPEAKING TO MIRANDA*

Caroline Macdonald is now one of Australia's most highly regarded writers for children – her books meeting with critical, popular and international acclaim.

Following the outstanding success of *The Lake at the End of the World* (recipient of many awards including: winner of the 1989 Alan Marshall Award; runner-up for the 1990 *Guardian* Children's Fiction Award; Honour Book in the 1989 Children's Book Council of Australia Book of the Year Awards), *Speaking to Miranda* was shortlisted for the Children's Book Council of Australia Book of the Year Award, the New Zealand AIM Children's Book Award and was runner-up in the NSW Family Therapy Association Awards, all in 1991.

For the last ten years, Caroline Macdonald has divided her time between Australia and New Zealand and she is now living in Adelaide.

Of *Speaking to Miranda*:

'It's impossible to do justice to all the twists and turns, the subtleties and mysteries of Caroline Macdonald's wondrous and amazing book.'
Moira Robinson, *Australian Women's Book Review*

'with its sure characterisation and compelling plot it will undoubtedly draw readers hypnotically into the story'
*Magpies*

*BY THE SAME AUTHOR*

*Elephant Rock*
*Visitors*
*Joseph's Boat*
*The Lake at the End of the World*
*Hostilities*
*The Eye Witness*

# SPEAKING TO MIRANDA

## Caroline Macdonald

PUFFIN BOOKS

Puffin Books
Penguin Books Australia Ltd
487 Maroondah Highway, PO Box 257
Ringwood, Victoria 3134, Australia
Penguin Books Ltd
Harmondsworth, Middlesex, England
Viking Penguin, A Division of Penguin Books USA Inc.
375 Hudson Street, New York, New York 10014, USA
Penguin Books Canada Limited
10 Alcorn Avenue, Toronto, Ontario, Canada M4V 1E4
Penguin Books (N.Z.) Ltd
182–190 Wairau Road, Auckland 10, New Zealand

First published by Viking, 1990
This Puffin edition first published, 1992
10 9 8 7 6 5 4 3 2 1
Copyright © Caroline Macdonald, 1990

Typeset in 13/15 Bembo by Midland Typesetters
Made and printed in Australia by Australian Print Group

National Library of Australia
Cataloguing-in-Publication data:

Macdonald, Caroline.
  Speaking to Miranda.
  ISBN 0 14 034970 7.
  I. Title.
NZ823.3

Every effort has been made to trace copyright holders. The publisher
would like to hear from any owner not here acknowledged.

For E.W.

## CHAPTER 1

Miranda was always there. We talked to each other endlessly during long car journeys, or while standing on the fringe at strange new schools, or while lying awake at night waiting for the sound of Rob's car. She used to tell me things I needed to know. And Rob told me once that I was talking to her even during my mother's funeral: chattering in a two-year-old's nonsense language while the others there ducked their heads, embarrassed, and Rob put his arms around me, murmuring hush. I remember touching the tears on his face. No, I don't suppose I really remember that; probably Miranda told me. It was no shock when Rob got round to telling me he wasn't my real father. Miranda had told me ages before.

But this was years ago. I haven't spoken to her since I was thirteen, when her hostility hit me so hard I didn't know if I'd recover. Of course I recovered, and I managed to live without Miranda. All it required was learning how to ignore her.

It's not curious that I should be thinking about her

now. Scenes from childhood are bombarding me these days, haphazardly, bristling with details I thought I'd forgotten.

'You're very quiet, Ruby.'

Rob's behind me, reading the morning paper at the kitchen table. I don't know how long I've been standing at the open French doors, staring at the brick garden.

'I can't decide, Rob. I'm sick of thinking about it.' It's decision time. I'm eighteen. The exam results don't come out until mid-January, but I should scrape up enough marks to get into university. But which one and what to do? I've thought about taking architecture and meteorology so I could keep working in Rob's business.

I know Rob would like that, but he's not pressuring me. He's always been the same: an uncritical ally. 'Don't rush into anything,' he says. 'Take a year off. Come to Darwin with me.'

Rob's a consulting architect who specialises in adapting houses to difficult climates. All my life we've been on the move.

'I don't know . . .' I shrug. Another unresolved conversation about My Future. Rob and I leave the house and walk to the corner deli for cappuccino and croissants. It's early summer, a sunny Melbourne morning, warm enough to sit outside at a table on the pavement. A breeze ruffles Rob's longish light-brown hair. Long hair suits his bony face, but I know he'll get it cut when he goes into the heat up north. I was only seven when we were in Darwin last. I get a sudden memory of the hot morning winds in the dry season.

'I'd be glad if you did come to Darwin,' Rob says. 'You know the job and it's easier for me to have you than to employ some stranger when I get there.'

'Oh, yeah. That's just because you can't get anyone else to do the dogsbody work. Photocopying plans and dropping them off at builders and surveyors. Organising the porta-loos.'

'Not true, Ruby-baby. You're a full partner, as ever. Summerton and Daughter.'

'Why not Summerton and Summerton?' I tease. 'Or even Summerton and Blake?'

I wish I could kill the words as soon as I've said them. He gets that stillness in his face, that frightening withdrawal from me. Emma Blake was my mother and after all these years I should have learned not to say her name to him.

'Rob, I'm sorry – '

He smiles; he's back with me again. 'Promise you'll give the trip to Darwin some thought.'

'Oh, yes, I will – I promise.'

Later I phone Alex. 'Look, Alex, I don't really feel like coming round tonight. I've got a lot on my mind just now. Let's leave it till tomorrow night, okay?'

'You know what, Ruby? The trouble with you is you have a lot of moods, you know that? You've always got excuses. Always something's wrong.'

'Alex! That's not true. All I'm saying is – '

'All you're always saying is that you'd rather not be with me. Right. Okay. So be it.'

'Don't go all paranoic on me, Alex. Of course I like seeing you – '

'Well, come on then. Or would you rather do a pub and hear some music?'

'Yes, Alex, I would but just not tonight, okay? Tomorrow maybe.'

'I might be busy tomorrow.'

'Look, I'm thinking of going to Darwin with Rob for a while.'

'Darwin. Well, that's just great. Just great, that's what that is. Have a great time.' The phone at his end goes clunk. He's hung up.

I usually like being at Alex's place, and I know he wants me to move in there with him. It's a big flat above an empty shop in Fitzroy that he shares with two and sometimes three others. They know they can't stay there much longer as they see premises on each side and across the road become designer outlets and brave new styling salons and restaurants whose smells of cooking drift up the stairs. There's lots of talk about our starting a business in the shop below, but what? None of us have training or talent or capital.

There's a murmur from the phone in the living room and I turn towards it hopefully but it's only Rob ringing out from the extension in his study. Anyway, I know Alex won't ring back after his sarcastic words. The next move will have to be mine.

If I don't go to Darwin it will be the first time Rob's gone anywhere without me.

I remember Miss Burton, a teacher I idolised, talking to Rob when I was six years old. 'Can't you find someone to care for Ruby while you're in Darwin, Mr Summerton?' She was tall with smooth grey hair and a calm voice. She rarely smiled. I must have been eavesdropping because I can picture her in the classroom but I can't picture her with Rob. Perhaps Miranda reported the conversation. 'Someone in the area, so she can continue her schooling here. She must have some continuity. Besides which, surely it's not a good idea to take her to Darwin? Conditions there are still difficult after the cyclone, I hear . . .' I immediately disliked Miss Burton.

Rob's reply didn't comfort me. 'I'll certainly consider it. I'll let you have a decision in a day or two.'

In a moment he was in my room. 'Got your bag packed yet?' he demanded. 'What's all this hanging around doing nothing? Summerton and Daughter are supposed to be away in half an hour. Do I have to do everything for you, Ruby-baby?' He tossed woollen jumpers into a corner and sorted out cotton shorts and tops. I was quivering with relief.

A day or two later, when he was supposed to be telling the teacher his decision for my future, we were settled in Darwin. That is, as settled as it was possible to be early in 1975, so soon after Cyclone Tracy.

Miranda was there. She was always there when I was on my own. We went from the tropical heat of Darwin to a chateau on the slopes of a mountain. The wind howled and there were snow blizzards. Rob was advising on the design of a ski resort. I spent hours huddled in front of an open fire whose heat disappeared before it reached half-way across the room. The cold bored through the thin outer walls. Miranda helped me invent colds and sore throats so I wouldn't have to shiver in the bus to the local school where the kids despised me because I couldn't ski. I became a very good liar under Miranda's guidance.

But then I realised that Rob was starting to worry about me. He was muttering about sending me away from the chateau back to Gran's in Melbourne. I started catching the bus to school, and I learned how to ski. Life suddenly got better. But Miranda was away for days at a time. Only once, during a day when every time the squalls of wind stopped I could hear a baby crying on and on somewhere in one of the rooms of the chateau, I caught a trace of her voice. *You cried*, she said, *every minute until you were one year old.*

I shake my head to force my thoughts back to the present. Why do I start daydreaming about the past whenever I try to make a decision?

The day's turned cooler. I decide to get a jacket and go round to Alex's. My hand hovers by the long black cape hanging in the wardrobe. My prized possession.

If I go to Darwin I wouldn't have to take much with me. We'd be going into the wet season. A sarong or two will be all I'll need. I could give Alex my cape as a sort of don't-hate-me present. He's borrowed it three or four times and already thinks it's half his.

Rob's stopped talking on the phone. I push open the door of his study.

'Why don't you book me on that flight to Darwin with you, Rob?'

He swings around in his big leather chair towards me. 'Good on you,' he says, his face full of approval.

## CHAPTER 2

Alex couldn't believe that I was serious about going to Darwin. His black eyes grew huge in his thin dark face, and right then his face looked sharper than ever because his hair was savagely pulled back into a ponytail. He wouldn't let me touch him; he wouldn't talk to me; pretended I wasn't there and left me sitting on the floor while he laughed with the others about something else.

Later I shouted at him. He softened and mumbled he loved me and everything seemed back to normal. I know he thinks I'll change my mind, I'll stay in Melbourne. But it's too late now. I like too much the relief of having finally made a decision, whether it's right or wrong.

I'm standing in the doorway of Rob's study, stroking the soft black fabric of my cape. Rob pushes past me with a carton of cassettes and CDs. 'I thought I'd give this to Alex,' I tell him, swinging the cape.

He puts the carton on his desk slowly and turns to look at the cape. 'Put it on,' he says.

'Oh, Rob, in this heat?' But I drape it over my shoulders and turn around a couple of times, feeling the heavy fabric swirl out and in to brush my bare ankles. 'I'd never be able to wear it in Darwin.'

'You won't be in the tropics for ever. You might need it again. Why don't you give him something else?' Rob touches the carton of recorded music. 'These, for instance?'

'Alex likes the cape. I feel guilty about going. Sort of.' I fling the cape across the back of Rob's chair and admire the way its folds still swing.

'Keep the cloak.'

'Why?'

'It looks good on you.' He's fiddling with papers on his desk as if this conversation means nothing.

'You're the one, Rob, who's always said don't get hung up on possessions.' He's not only said it, he's made it necessary because every six or seven months he lands a new contract somewhere else in Australia and we move again. I've accumulated very few treasures, and neither has he. Except this house in Melbourne, and I know why that is.

'I'd like you to keep the cloak,' Rob says with his voice muffled because his face is almost inside a carton of books, 'because Emma had one exactly like it.'

I hear the words and feel my palms tingle. I remember the way Rob looked when I brought the cape home and swirled through the house in it, showing off.

'Nice,' he'd said, and disappeared into the study, appearing uninterested. Too excited to take much notice, I'd rushed around to prance at Alex's.

This is the first time Rob has mentioned my mother's name of his own volition, without my questions; but then, I haven't questioned him directly about her for years.

Rob's still watching the cloak. I grab the opportunity.

'What happened to Emma's things?'

'She didn't have many,' he answers at last. 'A few clothes, and the cloak. Most of the rest were the things she needed to look after you. Your toys, baby clothes . . . When I finally came back here to live, Emma's possessions had gone. Mum got rid of them. That's why I got a hell of a shock when I saw you wearing that cloak. But I suppose it's a classic design. Remember the movie of *The French Lieutenant's Woman*? What's-her-name standing on the pier with the stormy sea all around and the wind whipping at her black cape?'

I nod.

'We'd seen the video just a few months before. I calmed down and realised that was probably why you'd chosen that cloak. You couldn't possibly have remembered Emma's.'

Sixteen years since she died, and I suspect not half a day goes by when he doesn't grieve for her. 'Okay, Rob, I'll keep it. I really wanted to all along.' I watch him for a minute before leaving the study, but his eyes are fixed on the window beyond his desk, and I know he won't say any more.

Later in the afternoon I phone Alex. 'I'm coming over. See you in ten minutes.'

'What for?' he asks.

'What do you mean, what for? To see you of course, and say goodbye and things.'

'So you really are going.'

'Alex, it's not the end of the world. I won't be there for ever – I'll be back, and we can write and phone while I'm away . . .' There's a long pause. 'Alex?' I hear a sigh.

'I'd rather we didn't write and ring up and so on. If you're going you're going and that's it. And I don't like goodbyes. So don't come round, Ruby. Bye.'

'Alex!' I shout, but there is only the buzz of a disconnected line.

I dial his number again but get a busy signal, and hang up quickly in case he's ringing me back. The phone here remains silent. I ring Alex again; again the busy signal.

I didn't expect this. I'd envisaged emotional tender farewells when he came to see me off at the airport. I'd wanted to get letters I could read over and over and get moody about.

I go and tell Rob. He puts his arm around my shoulder. 'Poor Ruby-baby. It's still up to you, you know. You can change your mind, stay here, if you wish.'

I tell him I'll think about it.

Rob goes out later in the evening. My self-esteem is suddenly so low I say to him as he leaves that if there's someone he'd rather take in my place . . . I'd understand . . . He tells me not to be silly.

I drift about the house during the evening. All my confidence that I've made a good decision to go to Darwin with Rob has gone. Occasionally I try Alex's number. It's always engaged. I can't believe someone's using the phone non-stop. I think about going to see Alex, not waiting to telephone him first, but I don't have the nerve. I can't do that unless it's to tell him that I've changed my mind about going away.

It's countdown time now until the plane leaves early tomorrow morning. Our bags stand in the hallway by the front door, with cabin bags still open ready for last-minute things. The box of cassettes and CDs is by the door where I'd left it ready to take to Alex's. For a moment I consider having it delivered to him anyway to make him feel bad. I decide not to, and move it with vicious kicks along the carpet to Rob's study and boot it under the desk.

There's the cloak, draped over Rob's chair. I hold it up, looking at the gold silky lining shimmering in the light thrown by the desk lamp, remembering Rob's words: *Emma had one just like it.* He's seen me wearing it for six months and said nothing about it until today. It pleases me, the coincidence of choosing something like Emma's. The cloak wasn't new when I bought it. It looked in good condition, hardly worn at all. But I know that clothes like this can last for years.

It's crazy, this direction my brain's taking. I don't try to stop it. Five minutes later I'm in a cab, giving the driver Gran's address.

Gran's surprised to see me; we'd said our goodbyes last night. But only a little surprised. Gran's vague these days. A minor stroke has collapsed her left eye slightly and she's forgetful.

She hugs me. 'I thought you'd already gone. Have you got Rob with you?'

'No, Gran, I came in a taxi.'

'Come in and have a little sherry. You can watch some TV with me.'

'Gran, look, I came to ask something in particular.' I notice the slight alarm on her face that's been there ever since her stroke when she feels there's going to be a matter that needs dealing with.

'It's about Emma,' I continue. 'You remember after she died and Rob and I came to stay with you? When I was only two?' She nods. 'And you cleared out Rob's house and bundled up all of Emma's things?'

'Yes. I thought it would be easier for him if I did that. Poor boy, he was so distraught.' She frowns. 'Except the jewellery. I kept that for you and you've got it, haven't you?'

'Yes.' There was a gold chain from a fob watch, a plain gold ring, and a pair of jade earrings. 'Gran, what happened to the rest of the things?'

She shakes her head. There's a silence. 'Do you know, I can't remember. There wasn't much. I don't think I'd have thrown it away – not so soon. Of course there was nothing, nothing at all to help us find out who she was, where she came from.'

'Perhaps you stored them somewhere in your old house?'

'Maybe. There was a lot of old stuff in the attic that had been there for years and when Rob's father died

I didn't have the heart to sort through it. When the house was sold, I guess it went with it.'

'Do you remember anything like this cloak, Gran?' I stand up and hold out the cloak I've slipped off my shoulders in the warmth of the centrally heated room. She touches it.

'Good quality,' she murmurs. 'I've noticed you wearing it a few times. And of course Emma did have a cloak very like that one.'

'I got it from a shop in Toorak Road called Labels Matter. Do you know it?'

'Now I can tell you about that shop.' The strained look she gets when she's aware of her failing memory disappears. I catch sight of the younger Gran – the elegant wealthy woman who knew everything there was to know about the inner circle of the city. 'It's the place where the sort of woman who wouldn't be caught dead wearing the same thing twice takes her clothes to sell them. Of course those women wouldn't actually buy anything there. Who knows but they mightn't meet the seller at the next cocktail party? But the sale offsets the cost of the next two-thousand-dollar dress. You know, a kind of seriously up-market op shop.'

I take a sip at the golden Spanish sherry. Possibly the buyers of Gran's old house went through the stuff and sold it and somehow this cloak found its way to Labels Matter.

I know I desperately want to believe this is Emma's cloak. On the way home in the cab I consider going to Gran and Pop's old house and asking the new owners how they got rid of the things in the attic. I could show them the cloak to see if they recognised it. It's too late tonight to do that. If I go to Darwin, there won't be time in the morning.

Alex. In the last hour or two I'd forgotten him.

When I get home I phone him again. Busy signal. I pace about, not knowing what to decide. The house seems cold. I stand in front of the long mirror, my cloak wrapped around me, its hood shadowing my face.

After a silence lasting five years, I speak to Miranda. *Of course*, she replies. *Of course it's Emma's cloak you're wearing.*

## CHAPTER 3

W e're on the flight to Darwin. The plane's half empty. Rob's reading all the morning newspapers and even though we're in business class the seats aren't wide enough – I have to dodge when he snaps the paper open to turn to the next page. So I move to the row of seats behind, and stare down at the miniature landscape. The untouched emptiness of the land beneath us rolls out to haziness at each horizon, and the busy sprawl of Melbourne suburbs we flew over only a few hours ago seems to be from another world. As the plane starts to descend slowly towards Alice Springs and I'm swallowing to stop the pain in my ears, he comes to sit beside me.

'Glad you came?'

'Don't know.'

'You're thinking about Alex?' Rob pauses. 'I know you think you've hurt him by deciding to rush off. And he's hitting back at you the only way he can, to hurt you in return. Looks like it's working, too.' I continue looking down at the red barrenness. 'You can write to him. He'll have had time to calm down a bit, mmm? Speak to me, Ruby-baby.' He shakes my shoulder gently. 'Look. You should remember that thing called emotional blackmail. Alex is a nice bloke and I don't suppose he'd be using it consciously. But my feeling is that if you'd given way to his pressure and stayed, you'd have been giving way to him for as long as you're together. Understand what I'm saying?'

'Thanks a whole lot, Rob,' I say sourly.

The cloak's in the overhead locker. I'd used the cold morning – typical Melbourne: nearly mid-summer yet there's a sudden cold snap and the early morning air stung like deep winter – as an excuse. It was too soon to part with it, now that I had found out it was Emma's. And another thing – something I was still feeling ambivalent about: the cloak had taken my mind off Alex for a while last night. Without its influence I might have stayed.

Forty minutes to fill in at the airport at Alice before the onward flight to Darwin. Rob's working on some papers and sipping beer from a can enclosed in a polystyrene tinny-holder which shows a laughing crocodile saying 'Keep your cool in the N.T.'. The bar's filled with souvenirs of the Northern Territory: the tough life, the real Australia, the Outback. A tourist promotion video keeps me watching for a while. More crocodiles; a bright flash of colour as a million birds wheel across a billabong in Kakadu National Park; the eerie muted colours of an ancient cave painting at Ubiri Rock; some idiot in a new leather Akubra hat snuggling up to an evil-looking baby crocodile while tourists take his photo. The video ends. It doesn't matter. I'm used to whiling away time in airports. We're always flying somewhere it seems.

This time five years ago, almost to the day, Rob and I were flying to Hobart. I don't know why I think of it now; I've tried to avoid memories of that summer in Tasmania. Actually it started off very well. We'd been living in Sydney most of the year and a violinist from the symphony orchestra had become a big part of our lives. She seemed to move in gradually until suddenly it seemed she'd expanded to fill the whole house. She spread noise and movement and lived during the nights. At midnight or later she'd arrive sometimes with five or six other musicians hyped up after a concert and the house would rock with the noise. She wore black all the time and soon there seemed to be shoals of delicate black lacy things everywhere. *She won't last long*, Miranda said.

Certainly I admired her; the drama of her and her beauty. Once she stroked my cheek and said there were nice bones somewhere underneath that chubbiness, and I fasted for days. I adored her thin muscular hands which were never still.

But her constant excitability was a drain on Rob, I could tell. He wasn't working properly. There were rows, slammed doors and screaming. She'd play frantically – strident gypsy music – on her violin at five in the morning to infuriate him.

It seemed to me he was pleased when he heard about the Hobart project, as if it were an excuse to move on again, to leave her behind us. She saw us off at the airport, a scene of emotion and tragedy – perhaps I'd wanted an echo of that scene when parting from Alex. When the plane was airborne I sneaked a look at Rob to see how he was. He caught me watching him. He reached for my hand and we laughed. There was no need to talk about it. I had Rob to myself again, and it was December with no school for weeks and weeks. I'd learned from the violinist that I was in control of what I looked like – all these things together made me feel different that summer. I felt as if I were shimmering. Everything was fun.

A few times I went with Rob to visit the site for the new apartment block. There were the usual arguments with the developers as to how much clearing of the block there should be before construction began. 'Tight-fisted bastards,' Rob said. 'They want to level the whole site to save a few dollars and a bit of inconvenience for a bulldozer operator. Do they think people want to live in a desert?'

Most of the time each day I had to myself. I've never minded being alone. The only time I don't like it is when people feel sorry for me as if they think I should mind it. But then there was always Miranda.

That summer she was infected with the same *joie de vivre* I had. She was the wise and comforting voice I'd always known, but more. We made each other laugh more. She flattered me when I experimented with hair-styles and dared me to go to a salon and get a glorious new haircut. I can still remember it: one side short and the other curling and longer and streaked with colour: blond and red. I had to phone Rob to come and pay the bill before they'd let me leave the salon. He looked puzzled when he saw me and then went pale when he saw the bill.

Rob and I were living in connecting apartments overlooking the Derwent River, in Sandy Bay just a few streets south of the casino. Rob used his sitting room for an office and we shared the living-room part of mine. All the same, it felt as if I had my own apartment, my own key and telephone – although I didn't know anyone local to call. I had friends in other places but after the hair-salon incident Rob put a veto on interstate calls. 'I've got to draw the line somewhere,' he said. And then 'I'm not made of money you know', which he said from time to time. It always made me laugh because he said it vaguely, with little conviction; and when I'd heard it as a child I'd laughed because I could *see* he wasn't made of money. No piles of twenty cents for arms and legs, no thatch of five-dollar notes on his head.

It was an unusually hot summer in Hobart. I walked down to the small crowded beach near our apartment every day for a swim in the river. My pale skin turned rosy, then a dark honey colour. The bleached streaks in my hair became blonder.

Then, just before New Year, Richard arrived. He'd finished his first year of architecture and was to assist Rob for a work-experience project. In the morning of the last day of the year, Rob brought him to the apartment to look at plans on their way to the site.

I heard Rob explaining things and went into the office to see them. Richard was beautiful.

I decided to go with them when they visited the site. Rob wanted to continue instructing Richard so he put me in the back seat. I realised it meant I could go on staring at Richard unnoticed. His hair ended in dark feathers on the back of his neck and he wore one plain gold ear stud.

On site I stuck close by them. Neither noticed; Rob was used to me taking interest in his work and Richard was hanging on to his every word. I hardly listened to Rob's flow of words as he explained how the areas of bush that had been left standing would fit into the layout of the apartments, and how the realignment of the individual buildings from the original plan would allow optimum living comfort both in the summer and in Hobart's cold winters. I stood with them on the platform of a crane at the level of the proposed first floor while Rob pointed to the views of upstream Derwent River that every apartment would have.

'You should be dealing in real estate, Mr Summerton,' Richard said. 'You make me want to buy the whole block already.' I thought it was the most intelligent and charming thing I'd ever heard anyone say.

It was New Year's Eve. Rob was invited to a big party and I was going too, and so was Richard.

I spent a long time getting ready. I hadn't noticed the unusual silence from Miranda. 'How do I look?' I asked her.

*Stupid*, she said. *Your hair's frizzy.*

'There's not time to do anything with it!' I tried to scrunch my hair into strands with some water. 'Is that okay?'

Silence.

At the party there were other families with kids my age but I stayed with Rob's group which included Richard. I took Richard glasses of champagne. I still hadn't exchanged more than two words with him.

Midnight. Linked arms and 'Auld Lang Syne'. Everyone kissing. A hug and a kiss from Rob then I turned to Richard on my other side. My memory is that he looked into my eyes for a long time then slowly kissed me – a long hard munching kiss, both of his arms around me. My head, light already from champagne, took off.

That was the start of the days of trailing after Richard, and Rob of course, as they worked. I mostly forgot about Miranda – except now and then when I'd tell her about the significance of a particular glance from Richard and the meaning of his arm brushing my shoulder. No time to think about her lack of response.

One Saturday I was on my own. It was a day off for Richard, and Rob was at the yacht club. Miranda spoke to me, *Richard's on the beach*, and I knew immediately it was the beach near our apartments and I could picture him, bored, lonely, wondering where I was.

I changed into bathers and put on sunscreen oil to make my skin glossy and hurried to the beach. I saw him straight away. He wasn't alone. There were three other people – a girl and two guys I'd never seen before. One of the guys lay on his stomach on a beach towel, reading aloud from a book while the others laughed and said things like 'Oh, no, how gross' – I wanted to run and also stay, and hovering indecisively on the edge of the group I was seen by Richard in mid-laugh as he rolled to take another tin from the cooler behind him. His face straightened. 'Ah, hi,' he said.

The group turned to look at me.

'Hi,' I said. My voice squeaked.

There was a long silence. 'I've come down for a swim,' I started to say at exactly the same instant as Richard said, 'This is my temporary boss's daughter,' but the congruence of our voices wasn't funny as it usually is in those circumstances. It was simply awkward. Anyway the group wasn't looking at me. They were listening to Richard.

' – boss's daughter, um, sorry, I never did know your name.'

'Ruby,' I managed to say.

'Hi, Ruby,' one or two of them replied.

The guy who'd been reading propped his book against Richard's ribs. His sleek hair fell forward and some of its strands brushed Richard's skin. 'School will start soon, I guess?' he said. 'Back into the cage, huh?'

'Mmm,' I said. Already the other two were talking together, ignoring me.

'Well, bye then,' the sleek-haired one said.

'Bye.'

I stood in the river water a long time. There were bushfires in the hill suburbs north of Hobart. The sky darkened early and the air grew stifling. A single blackened gum leaf dropped into the water in front of me.

'Miranda?' No answer.

The group with Richard had left. I hurried back to the apartment, flooded with misery, aware of the tension of everyone around, seeing the people in anxious groups who watched the sky blackening with smoke from the fires in the northern suburbs.

Mount Wellington leaned even closer over us, the dramatic rocks at its crown tinged with dark orange, reflecting the sinister red-grey of the sky. The air smelt singed.

Gloom, gloom. A back-drop created just for me, for the tragedy that was my life.

I stood in front of the mirror in my room. *Silly haircut*, I heard Miranda telling me, *nose too big, neck too short, stooped shoulders, ugly girl. Nothing to say. Ignorant. Boring company.*

Shut up, shut UP!

Deliberately she'd sent me down to the beach to meet that misery. The next morning, as I stood on the terrace watching a sun swollen and red from the smoke in the sky rise over the river, she had more information for me. *Rob's very kind and all that to you. Of course he feels responsible. But do you really think he wants a kid dragging around with him all the time?*

And later, *Don't you think you should let him off the hook?*

At first her words were nothing compared with the agony of realising that Richard saw me as a kid whose name he'd never remembered. I went to the library a lot, punished myself by reading book after book from a shelf near the floor. Emile Zola was the author. One gloomy novel after another. I started eating junk again. Within days my jawbone disappeared and my huger chin sprouted zits.

Then Miranda's poison about Rob having to drag me around began to work. I wondered what to do. If I said to him, 'Am I a nuisance?', I knew him well enough to know he'd deny it. Gradually, as I reached the end of the library shelf, a plan was formed. I would say something like, 'Rob, I'm not sure if I want to keep on shifting about like this. It's hard, you know, changing schools, meeting new people. I want to go to uni eventually and I need some continuity of education . . .' I expected he'd jump at it, his blue eyes full of relief.

I rehearsed the statement on the way home from the library, eating a double-header gelati, even though I knew we were having dinner with new clients of Rob's. I was hungry all the time.

'Come on, Ruby-baby, best dress tonight. I need you to help me impress this lot. Hurry hurry – '

There was no time for me to tell Rob what I'd planned to. The best dress felt tight.

'Well,' said Rob later, as we drove back to the apartment, 'somehow between us we did the trick. Perth next week, what do you reckon?'

I couldn't answer. How kind he was, pretending like this that he automatically included me in his plans. I waited until the next morning to give him my rehearsed speech. He pretended he didn't believe me.

'But, Ruby-baby, I thought you liked travelling! I thought you were ready to move on. You liked it here at first, I know, but you've been bored recently, come on, admit it. You enjoyed living in Perth last time we were there. It'll be even better now – there's lots going on there over the next few years – ' He went on about exciting changes and reconstruction in Fremantle for the America's Cup and his theories about keeping a balance between preserving the atmosphere and providing amenities for thousands of visitors.

He was very convincing but worried, I could see, by my conviction that I should go back to Melbourne for my high-school years. I searched his face for signs of relief that he'd be freed of the need to look after me. I didn't know what to decide.

'You're jealous,' I raged at Miranda that night. 'You want to intrude between me and anyone I care about!'

*Jealous – of you?* I heard mocking laughter and was aware of a deep antagonism. *What are you? Nothing. The sum total of you is what I've made you. You are nothing – and will be nothing – without me. You'll always do what I want. I have created you, moulded you, and I can destroy you at any time.*

I was shocked and panicky. 'No, you can't! Get away from me, Miranda! I don't need you. Die!'

I went to Perth with Rob. For the first few weeks I couldn't help watching carefully, looking for signs that would prove he didn't want me around. There weren't any.

Because I liked reading and never had much trouble with schoolwork, shifting from school to school and sometimes missing whole terms never seemed to matter. Catching up was easy.

But I stopped speaking to Miranda. I decided to make that last exchange with her in Hobart a turning point for me, to a life without the interference of Miranda.

## CHAPTER 4

My Hobart memories have continued as we reboarded at Alice, as we've flown over the vastness of the Northern Territory as if fleeing from the Centre back to the edge, to a safe place for people to be. The plane starts the slow drift down to Darwin. I watch the smudges of small bushfires burning in the country south of the city. I see those, the drifts of white on the huge red-brownness; but it's as if I'm removed, still watching the video at Alice. I have a numbness from following deep tracks through disturbing memories.

Of course now I realise that even if Richard had noticed me, it would have been a bad move for him to start anything with his boss's thirteen-year-old daughter. And now I recognise that he wasn't interested in girls anyway. But I remember how much I hated Miranda for sending me to that humiliating scene on the beach.

It was the damage she nearly caused between Rob and me that made me hate her more. I wished her dead.

I wanted to kill her for making me nearly believe I was becoming a burden for Rob. Of course I wanted to stay with him and didn't want any other life from the one I'd been having. When I finally found the courage to say to him, 'Look, Rob, I'm afraid you're starting to find it a drag to have a thirteen-year-old daughter hanging around all the time,' he said, 'Of course it's not a drag. You're supposed to be with me. You're my family.' My reaction was that he'd have to say that, and perhaps he was just pretending, so much was my self-esteem crushed by Miranda's words. I couldn't tell him that Miranda was still in my life. He thought she'd long gone.

And, in the year that followed, it seemed she had. There were times I missed her, near panics at situations where previously she'd have guided me. There were times when I thought that by wishing her dead I'd truly killed her, and I felt aches of grief.

But these times grew fewer as the year in Perth continued. I remember it as a good year. I made friends and felt curiously free, independent, without Miranda's constant supervision, her judgements, her interference. And I was at last able to understand the reason I liked this moving around sort of life. Every place was a new start, a chance to present myself to new friends as any sort of person I wanted to be. This was even easier now that Miranda wasn't there bringing me always back to my old self.

So when, slowly, slowly, during my fifteenth and sixteenth years she turned up again, I resented her intrusion. I refused to speak to her. Generally I did the opposite to what she told me. I'd cast her as malicious. I expected her influence to be against my best interests.

The buying of the cloak was disturbing. Miranda was the obvious explanation. She'd taken me to that shop and dangled the cloak in front of my eyes and made me want it. It was like realising a whole new area of her influence over me. I remembered her words back in Hobart – something like 'nothing you do is without my direction'. She realised she could no longer steer me with her words so she'd been planting ideas in my head. Perhaps I had no volition of my own at all. Possibly even the words she told me directly were chosen knowing I'd do the opposite.

The plane has landed in Darwin. We're waiting for our luggage. 'Remember the last time we were here?' Rob's saying to me. 'Living by the wharves on the old *Patris*?'

I nod. I'm remembering too the sultry air, how people move comfortably, unhurriedly, dressed in shorts and thongs. My Melbourne clothes – black jeans, grey silky-knit jumper tucked firmly in at my waist – seem fussy and dull and hot.

A friend of Rob's meets us and drives us to his house near the beach at Nightcliff where we'll be staying for the first few nights. He takes the longer route alongside the coast. The strong blue of the sea is familiar, but streets which twelve years ago were gulfs of ruin are now lined with comfortable houses. Everywhere there's lush tropical greenness, leaves and fronds and flourishing creepers glistening from a recent rain-storm, seeming to sparkle with vigour and pleasure in this abundance of tropical heat and rain. Grey Melbourne at seven o'clock this morning seems very far away. Slowly my gloom is lifting.

'It's still the best house in Darwin,' Dave, Rob's friend, is telling him. 'You certainly know your trade, old mate.'

It's a big house, made of two double-storey blocks. Between them there's a paved courtyard shaded by palms and the wide verandahs all along the upper floor. I remember standing on the empty land, those years ago, while Rob paced out the area for the foundations. Back then the beach across the road was strewn with debris from the cyclone still being washed up by every tide.

It's mid-afternoon. Dave takes us upstairs to our cool shady rooms with the brass ceiling fans, and I am asleep in minutes.

I'm wakened hours later by the sound of the shower running in the bathroom between our rooms. Soon I hear Rob's voice. 'Are you awake, Ruby? There are drinks and eats down by the pool.'

'Coming,' I shout back. I shower, wind on a sarong and go downstairs towards the sound of voices.

'Wow, look at that, a suntan!' someone says. 'You sure picked the worst time to come to Darwin. Can't swim at the beach because of the stingers, can't get a suntan because it's too hot.'

'It's all Rob's fault,' I say. 'We're always going to places in the worst possible weather.'

Everyone laughs and Rob spreads his hands in mock apology. 'Come and sit down, Ruby,' the girl continues and pats the chair beside her.

'You're Kate, aren't you?' I ask. I remember her from when I was six or seven. Kate had been eight then, and her older sister Evie, about ten. They'd intimidated me, and Miranda told me that Kate and Evie laughed at me behind my back.

As I look at Kate now I realise she's hardly changed. Katey Bear, she'd been called then, because of her sandy blondness, her stocky frame with short rounded arms and legs. Here she is now, a grown-up version, her hair longer and allowed to fall where it will in a tumble of blond and red curls.

'God, yeah, the heat's bloody,' someone else says. 'I never know why I bother coming home for Christmas. You can't move.' It has to be Evie. She has shiny golden hair cut very short and elaborately made-up eyes.

'You come back here because you're dying to see us all,' Kate replies to Evie. 'Anyway you never do move when you're here. You spend half the time in the pool and the other half asleep.' Evie acknowledges Kate's remark by no more than a slight lift of one perfectly shaped eyebrow. She doesn't acknowledge me at all.

I meet the others lounging around the table by the pool and drink long glasses of icy water laced with lime juice. Mostly I talk to Kate. She laughs when I tell her about being intimidated by her and Evie. 'And here were we,' she says, 'thinking you were a snooty little kid and secretly dead jealous of your exciting life travelling round all the time. And of course we were envious that you lived on the *Patris*.' She tells me about her work at a drop-in centre for kids. 'I can't leave Darwin,' she says. 'I love living here. Unlike Evie. She got away as soon as she could.'

I look towards Evie. Kate's easy to get along with and already I know we'll be friends. But I still feel intimidated by Evie. She's no more than four years older than me, and yet she projects nearly a generation of superiority over me. Perhaps I'm imagining this. She's scarcely noticing I exist. But I'm certainly noticing how she's monopolising Rob. She can't take her eyes off him.

We decide to stay on at Dave's house until after Christmas. I slide into this peaceful life of not moving too fast, seeking out the shade, avoiding the sudden deluges of tropical rain, sipping on icy water. There's a day before Christmas when Kate drives me into the city. I'm supposed to be buying sandals or thongs but the effort of taking shoes on and off is just too great. We wander down to the gardens by the esplanade and collapse on the grass under a tree, looking at the harbour – bright turquoise turning dark at the horizon where it meets boiling black clouds.

Kate's making me feel at home, secure. Perhaps she's even mothering me a little. She has a comfortable air of being immensely at ease here, lolling on the grass in loose jungle print shorts, her skin and hair glowing. She makes me feel scrawny, undernourished,

*33*

weak, instead of the usual lean and racey image I now have of myself. Her whole presence seems to reassure me that she'll make sure I don't starve or snap in half . . .

'Will your mother be back for Christmas?' I ask.

'Perhaps. Hope so. She drops in and out without much warning usually. Kinda unpredictable, our mum.'

'Do you miss her?' It's only an idle enquiry and I'm jolted by Kate's strong reaction.

'Of course I do! What a question. I'm used to her being away, I suppose, but when she's here I hate it when I see that vague bored look she gets when she wants to go back south. It's awful.' Then Kate rolls over and looks at me. 'I'm sorry, Ruby. I wasn't thinking. Your mother died, didn't she, when you were really young?'

'When I was two. You could hardly say I knew her. It's not as if I know what I'm missing. Then there's always been Rob.'

'Yeah, well, he's a great guy to have as a father.'

'He is. Well, you know he's not really my father. He's my step-father. He adopted me after my mother died.'

Kate's eyes are so round with surprise I nearly laugh. 'Really?' she says. 'So who's your real father?'

'Don't know.'

'You don't know? How come?'

I shrug. 'I suppose I don't know because Rob doesn't know.'

'And you've never tried to find out?'

'I wouldn't know where to start. Even if I wanted to. It seems a bit irrelevant.'

Kate's looking at me as if I'm from another planet. 'You're really not curious about him? Surely Rob would know who he is. Where was your mother from?'

'I don't know.' Now she's sure I'm from another planet, I can tell.

'I can't believe how you can be so – so uncurious. What do you know about her?'

'Almost nothing. Her name was Emma Blake. I used to have a photo of her. It was while we were here last time, living on the *Patris*, that the photo of Emma was stolen. Most of what I know I've heard from Rob's parents but they didn't know her long. I know you think it's crazy but what you don't understand is that I just can't question Rob about her. He gets upset. Too painful for him. He's never got over her.'

'He gets upset? Good grief, Ruby, he's got no right to keep information from you about your own mother.' She's gazing at me as if she'd like to shake sense into me.

At times I've wanted desperately to know more but I've turned back at the stone wall of Rob's grief. Caring too much for him, I've let the subject drop. I try to explain this to Kate.

She's unconvinced. 'It seems to me that's carrying grieving to absurd lengths. What is it now – nearly twenty years?'

'Sixteen.'

'Well. Even so.'

'How do you know it's too long to grieve? Has anyone you know ever died?'

'No. But anyway, that's no argument. That's like saying you can't have an opinion about apartheid unless you've been to South Africa.'

'It's not at all the same. It's quite different.'

'Well, go on then, why's it different?' Kate's grinning at me. I'm supposed to think clearly in this heat?

'All right. It's different because one's a personal emotion which you haven't felt and anyway the emotion might vary from person to person; and the other's a rational decision about a well-publicised political system.'

'Exactly. Well-publicised – but whose publicity do you believe unless you've been there?'

I'm confused for a moment. Then I have her. 'You're proving my point!'

'I know.' She's laughing. 'Got you going for a while, though, didn't I?'

I'd like to hit her but it takes too much energy to move. And I can tell she's purposely steered us away from a subject she thought might be getting too personal. Or perhaps she thought her own reaction might have been too strong. Anyway, she doesn't question me further, but her words hang around my thoughts for days.

Maybe she's right to think there's something bizarre about my lack of curiosity. Perhaps I've been wrong, cowardly, not to question Rob more firmly. But I'm not sure that words like right and wrong are appropriate here – after all, I reason, if you love someone you accept their oddities and it seems I have always accepted Rob's reticence over Emma. Kate simply doesn't understand that the bond encircling Rob and me makes up a family that is sufficient for both of us. And I decide to leave it there, and try not to think about it any more.

On Christmas Eve we all go dancing. There's Kate and some friends of hers, Rob with Evie hanging possessively on his arm, and Dave. Dave grumbled all day, saying he was past the age to be jiving about in some run-down Darwin sleaze-joint on Christmas Eve; he comes with us anyway and seems to know half the people there. Kate introduces me to James, a writer who's doing research on Darwin in the year after Cyclone Tracy for a film. He's interested when he learns I was here with Rob during 1975 and living on the *Patris*.

'Come round to the house tomorrow afternoon,' Kate tells him. 'You and Ruby can have a chat – Ruby can tell you what she remembers.'

'I remember hardly anything,' I protest. 'I mean, I was only six or seven.' It's not quite true. Even though Darwin looks so different now, memories are coming back with intensity. And then I get another reminder. When we get home around two-thirty there's Kate's mother, Jan, back from Sydney, waiting up for us by the pool.

I remember her vividly. She'd been a warm welcoming figure in our first weeks in Darwin when Rob seemed to be working all the hours in the day. I watch her hugging her family and recall clinging to her when Rob brought me on shore. She'd been a refuge while I was still finding life on the boat strange. With a slight shock I recall, too, that I'd told her about speaking to Miranda. She's the only person I've told, apart from Rob, of course. And perhaps Gran, but she'll have forgotten.

Memories. Even though I'm dead tired and dawn's not far away, I lie awake like I often did on the *Patris*. But in those days I had Miranda to talk to.

# CHAPTER 5

Spending a lifetime moving to new places meant I'd be asked over and over where my mother was. From when I was tiny I heard Rob's brief reply 'I'm a widower' and I quickly learned to say that she had died when I was very small and that now I lived with Rob who was my father. Questioners always responded with brief sympathetic silences and then talked about something else. Kate was the first to prolong the questioning.

'We're going to be living on a ship, Ruby-baby,' Rob told me as we were making our dash to Darwin all those years ago. 'Imagine, a beautiful cruise-ship with cinemas and dance halls and restaurants and dinky little cabins with portholes.'

I was confused. I thought we were going to Darwin to live for a while, not to go sailing across the sea. Rob explained that there was nowhere else for us to stay in Darwin, that all the houses had been pushed over in the cyclone. I couldn't believe this – a whole town flattened? It wasn't until we arrived that I understood what he meant. Everything was splintered, twisted, smashed, trampled as if by a marching army of giants.

The ship was crowded. At first I was overwhelmed by its noise and action twenty-four hours a day. I went with Rob as usual on his consultancy trips, but sometimes the sites he visited were still dangerous and unstable and I spent hours waiting for him in the hot landrover. Miranda's company helped, but even so there were long lonely days.

Then Rob became friendly with Dave and Jan, Kate and Evie's parents. They were living in a tiny prefabricated hut set beside the wreckage of their former house. I was shy of Evie and Kate. At this time I was relying more than ever on Miranda.

'Have you made friends on the ship yet, Ruby?' Jan asked one day when I was hanging about watching her work at something, mending a chair perhaps. Everyone was mending or building those days. That's when I told her about Miranda, who'd come with me from Melbourne and had always been my friend. Jan looked surprised – she'd known us for a few weeks by this time, and there'd always been only Rob and myself. But she didn't laugh or say anything about phantom playmates or invisible friends, and I don't think she ever told anyone else.

One night I overheard the adults talking. They thought I was asleep. Jan said something like 'You should tell Ruby soon'. It was hearing my name that got my attention. I felt nervous, wondering if she was going to tell them about Miranda. Even at that age

I knew Miranda's existence wasn't for just anyone to know. Jan's voice went on. 'I really believe, Rob, that the younger they are when they find out they're adopted, the easier it is for them to accept. They take it for granted. They see it as quite normal.'

'You're probably right,' I heard Rob say. He sounded worried. There was a pause. 'But not yet. I'd rather wait till she's more settled here.'

'Why don't you let her stay on the ship more?' That was from Dave. 'She'd get to know kids her own age. There are those supervised groups during the day for the workers' kids.'

'She likes coming on the rounds with me and at least I know she's safe. Perhaps going to live on the ship was a mistake. It seemed ideal because there'd be no hassle about cooking and laundry –'

I heard Jan laugh. 'My information is that you're the best cook in the world!'

'Yes, well, the odd crab soufflé, a camembert chicken –' The conversation droned on to food and how bad the vegetables were here and I was left wondering why Rob had sounded uneasy and worried about me. I was okay. I didn't want anything to change. I didn't want him to send me away or give me to somebody else.

Of course in time I made friends on the ship. Now I remember those days as endless fun, games from dawn through to the hazy red sunsets. I could tell Rob was pleased I was having a good time. When at last he found accommodation on shore for us, he gave in when I begged for us to stay on the ship.

He'd finished most of his government projects and was concentrating on designing Dave and Jan's new house, the one we're staying in now. 'It's going to be the best house in Darwin,' he told them. 'Absolutely perfect for the tropics.' It was about this time that he told me he wasn't my real father, that he'd adopted me legally after Emma died. I recognise now the apprehension with which he gave me the information. I don't know what he was afraid of. I loved him more than anything in the world and never once doubted his love for me. Real father or not real father didn't have much meaning for me. Anyway, Miranda had somehow got this information across to me a long time before, so it wasn't new news. My main feeling was relief that nothing was going to change, that he wasn't going to send me away.

And a few days later the awful thing happened. My cabin was burgled. It was my fault. I forgot to lock it one day in my rush to catch up with something that was happening on deck. I didn't even have anything worth stealing, but the green wallet where I kept my allowance and the photo of my mother was emptied, and everything else thrown on the floor. It had been a black and white photo of Emma, sitting on the beach with the sun throwing pools of blackness on her face. It was the only one I had.

I sat on my bunk, crying, in the middle of the mess. Miranda comforted me for a while. Then she said I was stupid to leave my cabin unlocked. *You've lost your mother and it's your fault*, she said.

These memories were buried deep. They affect me

more than any of the other pieces of past life I've been reliving recently. It's that one vivid recollection that moves me most, the pillaged cabin, the frantic search for the stolen photograph of Emma, my final acceptance that it was gone for ever and that it was my fault.

But now it's Christmas Day, and James the script researcher has turned up. These intensely personal memories are not what I want to tell him, and probably he's disappointed. But we swim in the pool and make plans to meet the next day.

'I told him I wouldn't be able to remember much,' I say to Kate later that evening.

'Don't worry about it. I'd say he's more interested in you in the present than you in the past,' she replies.

I laugh that off. 'I can't stand people with big black specs and hairy arms and he's so earnest. And what about the way his specs slide down his nose in the heat and he keeps on pushing them back with his finger?' Of course I know James is interested. I remember I've rarely given Alex a thought, not even written to him as Rob had suggested. It's far from my imagined scenario of hanging out every day for a letter from him, sending back passionate tear-stained replies – 'I miss you dreadfully' . . .

'I've hardly seen you lately, Ruby-baby,' Rob says a few days after Christmas.

'I've hardly seen you. Not without Evie hanging around your neck.'

'Yes, well, she is a bit, a bit . . .'

'Determined?' I suggest.

'You could say that. Not that you can talk. Not with that James following you around like a demented rabbit.' Rob and I are having dinner alone, eating satés at a restaurant near the waterfront. The sky's filled with sunset colour, the palm trees etched in black against the red. 'Well, they're due to go back south, both of them. This is shades of things to come, you know. Just the two of us, abandoned, no one else to talk to.'

'So sad.' We smile and toast each other silently with our glasses.

'Holiday's over, for me, anyway,' Rob says. 'I'm seeing that bloke from the Casuarina Beach development tomorrow. What about you? Do you want to come with me? Got any other plans? Actually, you look tired. Is this lazy tropical life exhausting you?'

I shrug, turning over possible replies in my mind. Every night from Christmas Eve has been nearly sleepless for me. I'm haunted by the image of the small girl crying, holding the empty green wallet cupped in her fingers. I wake up in tears and then can't sleep again.

We're sitting so near to where we'd watched the old *Patris* sail away, eleven years ago, not so long before we'd packed and headed south ourselves. Rob suggested this evening together alone; it suits me. I need to talk to him.

'Remember the day the *Patris* left?' I start.

'Certainly. Why?'

'I've been thinking about that time a lot since we've been back here. It's amazing how much I remember.'

'That's probably because James has been getting you to think back. Using you for his research. Not love at all.'

I smile but I won't be distracted. 'Perhaps. A little. But,' carefully I choose words, 'the memories I've been having aren't the sort I want to tell him. For instance it was here you told me you adopted me after Emma died.' His eyes shift from mine and he sits very still. 'And it was on the *Patris* that I lost my only photo of Emma. Rob, I've never asked before, but do you have any other photos of her?'

'No.'

The single word carries a weight of meaning – keep off, stop asking, leave it alone.

'And if I don't?'

'Don't what?'

'Stop asking you about Emma.'

'You know why, Ruby. It hurts to talk about her.'

'Rob, it's sixteen years now since she died. That's sixteen times as long as the time you even knew her. Surely by now you can talk to me about her?'

'Ruby, please leave it.'

I've never gone this far before in questions about Emma. Long before this point I'd have quailed at the look of pain on his face and the sight of tension in his hands. I have to keep asking, as if this is the only way to exorcise the dreams.

'You always do this to me, Rob.' I reach over and touch the fingers clenched around his glass. 'Remember when we were flying up here before Christmas? Talking about Alex? You said he was using emotional blackmail on me to get me to do what he wanted. Well, I think you're using a kind of emotional blackmail on me, too. Always have. Using my fear that you wouldn't love me any more if I hurt you by asking about Emma.'

'That's not fair, Ruby.' He won't look at me. His voice is husky.

'You knew her for a year. I was too young to know her at all, but she was my mother. I've got a right to know who she was and where she came from and everything. You must understand I need to know. You've got no right to keep all that from me.'

He stands up, eyes cold. I'm shaking, my hands feel clammy. Perhaps I've gone too far. I've seen the uncompromising anger he's capable of but it's never been directed towards me, not once. I'm afraid he'll walk away from me now. I've damaged things between us beyond retraction. I realise the old mechanism of fearing to hurt him is working as it always has before.

'I've asked you, Ruby, please drop this subject.'

'Rob!' I say despairingly. 'Don't you see you're doing it again?'

Finally he sits down and looks at me for a long time. I almost think I've won. Finally he speaks. 'If you've had enough to eat, Ruby, perhaps we could leave now.'

I could easily panic. I fight to keep calm, because I don't know if another time I could recreate this courage. At that thought, it's as if I gain a kind of detachment from the scene; I'm looking on as if I'm uninvolved. Suddenly I see why Kate found Rob's reticence so extraordinary. What is it that Rob's so afraid of, really? Why can't he talk to me? I'm not an outsider. He knows he has my sympathy.

'You're treating me like an enemy, Rob.'

'That's not true, Ruby – '

I interrupt. 'I'm the one who's alive, and it's my mother who's dead.'

'I know Emma's dead.' Every word is bitter.

'Why don't you talk about her? What are you afraid of? It's not your fault she died.' He doesn't answer. 'Rob?' His eyes are black with hostility. The sharp angles of his face are turned to gauntness by the dim light.

'How long do you intend to persist with this questioning?' he asks quietly.

'Until you answer. I mean it, Rob.'

He stands up swiftly. 'I need a drink,' he says, and heads for the bar. He brings back a bottle of champagne and pours us each a glass. There are still waves of hostility from him. There's none of our usual glass-clinking ceremony. At last he speaks. 'What you don't realise is that I don't know much myself. What you've heard over the years probably adds up to the sum total of what I know. And that's part of the pain. Not knowing. Losing her without knowing anything about her.'

'But you did know her, Rob. You lived with her for a whole year. Don't you realise she's less than a shadow for me? I've got nothing . . .' This is when my tears really threaten. I blink them away, and swallow. 'Tell me it all, Rob. Start at the beginning. Where you

47

met her, what happened next. Tell me everything.'
Silence. 'Please.'

I don't know what it is that changes his mind. I'm
aware his hostility has gone, even his resentment, when
he speaks again. Perhaps, as I have, he detaches himself
a little. But still his voice is husky, reluctant.

'Appropriate,' he says, looking into his glass of
champagne. 'The first drink Emma and I shared.
Different circumstances, though – very.'

'What were they?' I prompt as he pauses.

'Well, you were there, not that you'd remember.
You were sound asleep in a bundle on Emma's lap.
Emma and I were wrapped in her cloak sitting on the
sand on the beach, watching a bonfire we'd built. More
accurate to say an unsuccessful little fire. Drinking
champagne and shivering and laughing at the piquant
flavour of salt the sand in our glasses gave the
champagne. Freezing cold night and crunchy champagne.' He laughs. 'I'd have eaten handfuls of sand in
a snowstorm to please her.'

'Go on.'

'Start at the beginning, you said. She was hitchhiking. I'd given her a lift. She said she had to get to
Melbourne, but I was staying down the coast with
some mates to do a bit of surfing. It was Easter '69.
The surf was biting that autumn. Good off-shore
winds. I felt sorry for her, hitchhiking with a little
baby, but not sorry enough to drive her all the way
to Melbourne then and there. Not at that stage,
anyway.'

'So what happened?'

'It was getting late in the day and cold, and you were snivelling, so I said why not come back to where I was staying. Plenty of room, and she could get an early start next day. Not safe to be hitching in the dark. I dropped her off at the house and raced off to get some surfing in before dark.' He pauses but I can see that now he needs no more prompting. He's tense, speaking quietly, as if this time he really wants to relive these scenes.

'When I came back, she'd showered and put on one of those long Indian muslin dresses and there she stood by the window, holding you. I guess I fell in love right then. I'm Emma, she said, and this is Ruby. I remember I could hardly speak. I think I said something dopey like hello, Ruby-baby and poked my finger at you. You laughed at me. Emma said you were one year old that very day. That was the night we went down to the beach and drank champagne.

'Then the next day it seemed easier that she stayed on till we went back to Melbourne after Easter and I could drive her myself. By then of course I couldn't bear the thought of her getting into some other guy's car, perhaps not seeing her again. The others looked sideways at first, seeing a baby turning up at the beach house, but you won them over. You were a good baby.' I remember fleetingly Miranda's comment that I'd cried non-stop until my first birthday. 'So, off we went to Melbourne. Arrived on Mum and Dad Tuesday night, me with a whole new family.'

'What did they think?'

'They didn't say a whole lot. But you know them, busy with their own lives.' He pauses. 'Perhaps, though, Mum did have a questioning look in her eye for Emma – but only at first. Anyway, we stayed there for a week or so and then shifted to the Fitzroy house. I'd finished uni and had a good job, but thinking back it seems a bit bizarre – one day to be sitting on a surfboard, completely free, and a week later having a family and a mortgage. But Emma had that way of making everything seem natural and right, as if it were meant to happen exactly as it did.'

'And then?'

'Then another Easter, another beach. You don't need me to tell you all that again, Ruby. Gran's told you, I know.'

I nod. 'But where had she come from when you picked her up hitching? Why was she heading for Melbourne?'

'I don't know. She never told me. And she didn't know anyone in Melbourne.'

'What did you talk about all the time? In a whole year, surely she said something about her past? Some clue?'

'We talked about the stars, politics, movies, everything but her past.'

'I can't believe you didn't have some curiosity. Like where I was born, about my father?'

'Well, yes, I did ask about you. Ruby-baby, you accuse me of being evasive about questions. I had a bloody good teacher in your mother about avoiding straight answers. She didn't tell me a thing. I didn't care. I thought she'd tell me when she was ready. I thought there was all the time in the world.'

I can see his sadness building up. One last question. 'What did she have with her when you met her? She must have had papers, cheque book, credit cards – something?'

'Let me tell you what she had. One pair of jeans, two black wool sweaters, high-heeled boots, sandals, one dress, some undies, a dying toothbrush and a hairbrush, a packet of disposable nappies and a couple of jumpsuits for you, a tatty koala also yours, and a crocheted woolly rug for you. And the cloak. And twenty-seven dollars. That's it. She was a mystery woman.'

I think of all the junk I cart around in my wallet. Library card, driver's licence, savings book, diary with every detail filled in on that front page, even my blood group. There's no mystery about me.

'So,' Rob is continuing, 'that's why it was so hard to know what to do after she died. I tried to trace her family, through the police, the births' registry, to find out about you, even put her photo in the paper. I tried hard, but I was relieved, really, when no one came to claim you away from me. You were all I had left of her.'

'Well, that photo of her in the sunlight – I remember it wasn't very clear.'

He looks down at his hands for a while. 'There is another photo. It's very clear. You can see her face in every detail. I've only seen that photo once. Perhaps your gran still has it. She looked after all that business after Emma died. The photo was taken in the morgue. A death mask, Ruby.'

I have no more questions. I link my arm through his, and together we walk slowly through the soft darkness to the car.

Perhaps her name wasn't Emma. Perhaps I'm not Ruby. Somewhere I might have another birth certificate with another name on it. But I want to be Ruby Summerton. I choose that name for ever.

## CHAPTER 6

I've been hit by anger towards my mother in the days since I talked with Rob. I resent her determination to obscure her past and leave me floating, nameless and unclaimed if it weren't for Rob.

Even though I've grown so close to Kate, I let a few days pass before I tell her about what Rob said. We're still staying at their house. By now the Christmas visitors have gone – Evie, and Jan; and James has returned to Adelaide. I've tried to get involved in the development Rob's working on but my heart's not in it. This makes me feel guilty. I'm closer to Rob than ever and I don't want to let him down. He's keen on the 'Summerton and Daughter' idea. I still don't know what to do with my life. Days drift by.

It's early afternoon. Kate and I have lazed in the pool and I've had my third shower of the day. I'm wearing a new sarong made of fine green and black Indian cotton, and the jade earrings that had belonged to Emma. I don't wear them often, probably out of concern for Rob's feelings. But they match my new sarong, and they put me in the mood to talk about Emma.

'He wasn't keeping anything from me. As he said, she was a mystery woman. An anonymous person.'

'She would have known who she was. And she must have had a husband or at least a lover or you wouldn't exist. She'd have parents, and he would have parents – somewhere there's a whole chain of people who knew her. Schoolfriends, dentists, teachers, endless acquaintances. Like we all have.'

'Okay, so why didn't any of them answer the ads in the papers?'

'It's hard to say. Ruby, you're sure Rob was telling you the truth?'

'Of course I'm sure.'

'All right, don't get in a fury. It was just a thought. You have to admit it's a strange story. All the same, I suppose it would be easy enough to achieve. Become an unknown new person.'

'How do you mean?'

'Well, you for instance. Here you are, sitting around twiddling your thumbs, trying to decide what to do with your life. Or even the next six months. Tomorrow morning you have a brainwave. I want to travel to Europe! you announce to Rob – or India, or Botswana or whatever. We wave goodbye at the airport as you fly off back to Melbourne to arrange your passport and so on. But you sneakily jump the plane when it lands in Alice and into the nearest garbage tin you dump your air-ticket, your credit cards and everything else that's got your name on it. Then you buy a bus-ticket to Brisbane as Jane Jones, Cassandra Cavanagh, Fiona Faulkner, Nelly Nobody. Simple.'

'It might work for a while. Until I wanted a driver's licence, or got sick, or ran out of money. And anyway, it wouldn't be long before Rob would try to find me.'

'If you were clever enough in covering your tracks, it wouldn't be easy for him.'

'And he'd certainly claim me if he saw my photo in the papers.'

'Yes, of course, in your circumstances. But just supposing he didn't want to claim you?'

I begin to comprehend where our conversation's heading. A woman disappears. No one tries to find her, or admits to knowing her when she's dead, even though she's survived by a two-year-old daughter.

'If I were to run away in the way you suggest,' I say slowly, 'leaving Rob and all of you and Gran not knowing or caring where I was, I would have had to have done something so awful that I couldn't face you all and you all wished me dead anyway. Disappearing like that is, well, one step short of suicide. It's desperation stuff. Oh, Kate, what do you think Emma could possibly have done? Murder?'

'Hey, Ruby, it needn't be anything like that. Look, there could be many explanations. Maybe she joined a religious sect and formally renounced her family and friends. Families can get pretty pissed off by that. Just think, Ruby, perhaps you're the offspring of a famous prophet.'

'Thanks a lot, Kate.'

'I wonder if your Gran still has that photo?' Suddenly she claps her hands, startling me. 'I have a wonderful idea. We can go to the State Library and look for it in the old papers.'

'No!' I'm panicked by the thought of it. 'Sorry, Kate, I don't want to. Anyway I'm a bit tired. I'm going to have a rest.'

'No you're not.' She stands up and tugs at my hand. 'You're not tired at all. You sleep half the time as it is. And I know you, you're just going to go on brooding about Emma and you've no hope of getting any answers by doing that. Come on. Action, woman.'

'But it's going to rain. Any minute.' Heavy clouds had gathered quickly and pressed the heat through the canopy of palm leaves.

'Ruby. There's a roof on the library, you know. And on the car. Come on.'

Kate does all the organising at the library. She asks for the microfilm for the Melbourne *Age* and the *Sydney Morning Herald* for 1970, and sets them up on two machines. 'There you are,' she says to me. 'I'll do the *Age*. When was it – around Easter? Zoom through to April, then.'

I'm almost paralysed. She's brisk and business-like but then it's not the death mask of *her* mother we're looking for. Like a zombie I spin the knob and watch the blur of newsprint on the screen. I can't focus, and anyway I don't expect this to lead anywhere. Almost I don't want it to lead anywhere. It's far too soon for me when Kate beckons.

'Come and look at this,' she says softly. She has focused on an article headlined 'Easter deaths by drowning exceed road toll'. Silently I read the paragraph she indicates.

A Melbourne woman drowned at South Red Beach in a brave effort to rescue an unknown swimmer. Her companion witnessed the rescue attempt from some distance away, but by the time he swam against the rip out to the scene he was too late to save the woman's life. Her name is being withheld until relatives are informed.

I nod. 'That's probably her.'

'So we're close to finding the photo,' Kate says. I sit down again. I have cramps in my stomach. Soon she starts reading in a quiet voice. ' "Friends of the woman pictured here, known as Emma Blake, aged about twenty-three, are seeking contact from her relatives. She arrived in Melbourne in April 1969, with no identification. She was accidentally drowned recently during an heroic rescue of another swimmer in difficulties. She is survived by a two-year-old daughter named Ruby. Anyone able to help is urged to contact either the police or Robert Summerton, 25 Elgave Crescent, Fitzroy, Melbourne, phone (03) 4176003, as soon as possible." Here's the photo, Ruby.'

I see it, then look away immediately. It's horrible. 'She was very lovely,' I hear Kate say. 'The photo's blurry on the film, but you can see she's definitely your mother. Look at her cheekbones, and the shape of her eyebrows.'

I can't look. Kate makes a print of the article and the photo, and stands looking at it critically. 'It's a terrible print, but the best we can get from microfilm. You'll have to see if your gran's got the original.'

We leave the library. Outside the heat hits after the air-conditioning, but the rain storm has passed and the air smells sweet.

'Why?' I manage to ask at last.

'Because, idiot, it's the only way you're going to find out who she was.' Kate glances at her watch. 'Look, Ruby, I've got to rush. My afternoon shift's about to start. You take the car home, okay? I can get a lift later.' She hands me the print from the newspaper. I fold it in half quickly. 'Sorry, Ruby.' She hugs me. 'It's all been a bit much for you, hasn't it? Don't hate me. Here're the car keys. Remember where we parked?'

She's gone. I go into the nearest cafe and order cappuccino and a glass of water. The folded page I leave on the table between the glass and the cup.

In the end I open the page and look at the photo. Her eyes are closed. Her face is a series of crescents: eyebrows, eyelashes, closed lips drooping slightly at each corner. Small ears. The photo is too indistinct to see what her hair was like. There seem to be a few wisps on her forehead. Either it's cut very short, or tied back behind her neck.

Suddenly the weight of my own hair, swinging forward over my ears and down my back, is unbearable. It's why I'm so hot. There are thirty-four dollars in my wallet. I pay for the untouched coffee, go to the nearest salon, and have it all cut off.

*

Rob and Dave are sitting in the shade, stubby-holders in their hands, the newspaper drifting away page by page in the breeze. Rob stares as I collapse on an empty chair beside him. Dave's not so silent. 'Who's this beautiful creature dropping in on us like a Sydney socialite? Friend of yours, Rob? Know any more like that?'

'Got too hot to carry round that much hair any more, Dave,' I tell him. 'Any more coldies around?'

'Sure are. Coke? Soda?'

'Beer.' I see him glance at Rob, but Rob's still staring at me. Dave shrugs and hands me a green one and a holder.

'New earrings, too? Very nice,' Dave goes on.

'Not new. I've had them for years. They were my mother's.' I unhook one and hand it to him. 'Jade.'

He holds it up. 'Yes. Very dark – New Zealand jade, I'd say. Greenstone. Interesting design, too – the sty-lised fish hook. A Maori motif.' Dave's a man in his fifties with a great beer gut who rarely wears anything but shorts and thongs and an old singlet and prefers jokes to any sort of serious talk, but he's a mineralogist and I've learned before that there's not much he doesn't know about stones of all kinds.

Rob speaks at last, his voice sounding controlled and level. 'It's a very nice haircut, Ruby. It took me by surprise. You look so different.'

'Well, at least I didn't have to phone you to come and pay for it,' I reply, trying to joke, hoping he'll smile, remember the Hobart haircut; but his face

remains expressionless. I get out the print from the
newspaper and smooth it on the table in front of him,
fighting to keep my hands steady so they won't betray
how very nervous I am. He looks at it for ages, then
back at me.

'You found it.'

'Yes. Has Gran got the original?'

'I don't know.' He seems to be still looking down
at the print, but when Dave reaches over and takes
it to read, Rob doesn't stop him or move his head.

'I want to try and find out who she was, Rob.'

'Ruby, I moved heaven and earth to do just that
sixteen years ago. I got nowhere. The cops got
nowhere. What makes you think you can do better
now?'

'I want to try.'

'Besides . . .' He hesitates and because of the
thoughts I had earlier about what dreadful thing she
might have done to want to disappear so thoroughly,
I know what he's going to say.

'You don't really want to know,' I finish for him.

'Perhaps. But anyway what can you do that hasn't
already been done? It seems hopeless. I know I can't
stop you – '

'You can, actually.'

'How?'

'Well, it'll take money. I've done nothing about
finding a job. I'm not even helping with your project.
I spent the rest of this month's allowance at the
hairdressers. I need a loan even to get a bus-fare if I
want to go out tomorrow.'

'How exactly are you proposing to go about this search?'

'I'll start by finding a better copy of that photograph, anyway.'

'And then advertise all over again?'

'No. It didn't work before, as you pointed out. It'll need a more personal job. Like a search.'

'You mean you're going to traipse all over the country with a photo that's sixteen years old? Well. You're right. It'll take money.'

'I'll work back from the point where you gave her a lift when she was hitching. I'm going to do it, Rob. If you won't help me I'll get any sort of job anywhere until I've got enough money to do it on my own.'

'Earrings might be a clue,' Dave says. I've forgotten he's there. He's still holding the earring I gave him. 'There's a distinctive style in the carving. And the engraving on the silver cap. You might track down the maker, anyway.' He continues. 'Nice quality. She must have had rich friends in New Zealand. Or made some money on a working holiday. Lots of Aussie girls pick up good wages doing a stint at the tourist hotels in the South Island.' Suddenly here's another dimension. A New Zealand connection.

'There, you see?' I turn back to Rob triumphantly. 'I'll bet you didn't put that ad in the New Zealand papers!'

It takes me two days of persuasion and argument to convince Rob I'm serious, that I won't give up this idea. In the end I force him into a kind of agreement. I can have a year for my search, and draw what expenses I need on Rob's credit card, provided that at the end of that year I return and work for him for two years or otherwise pay back the money over five years.

'You realise, don't you, that this is putting uni work far into the future,' he says to me.

I shrug. With this sudden obsession there's no way I could do uni work or any other kind. I phone and book a flight to Melbourne the next day.

*CHAPTER 7*

'Gran? It's me. Ruby. At the airport. Can I come and stay?'

Gran has been the most stable female figure in my life (apart from the dubious Miranda) even though sometimes years or months have passed without my seeing her. When I was about five, she showed me the jewellery that had belonged to Emma, telling me she'd looked after it for me but it was mine whenever I wanted it. I claimed it after the dreadful Hobart summer, before I turned fourteen. I remember trying on the earrings and asking Gran if Emma had been pretty. My self-esteem was damaged just then, and to find out I had pretty blood in my veins would have been a boost. There'd be hope for me, sort of thing, I suppose.

'Pretty?' Gran replied vaguely. 'I suppose so. She had style, knew how to dress.'

'Pretty?' wheezed Grandpa from his cane chair by the window. 'I'll say she was. Damned tragedy, thing like that to happen to a lovely girl in her prime.' Poor

63

Grandpa, too sick even then to leave the house to go to his beloved club, forced to let go the reins of his business enterprises, dead within six months from emphysema.

Gran has told me stories about going for tramps in the Grampians National Park with me in a carrier swapped around to each adult's back in turn. There were weekends at the beach and hikes up the You Yangs, the strange rocky hills leaping out of the plains between Melbourne and Geelong. 'She seemed to like us to be around,' Gran told me. 'None of this exclude-the-older-generation about her. She used to walk you over to visit us. She'd pick flowers that were poking over people's fences and thread them around the edge of your pushchair. You'd come up the path looking like a miniature float in a parade, garlanded with bougain-villaea and daisies and jasmine.' This is a strong image for me, sitting in a nest of flowers. It seems I can remember the smell of the jasmine. Perhaps it's my earliest conscious memory; more likely it's because Gran has alluded to it many times since I was little.

I've gleaned the possibility that Emma wasn't quite the sort of girl they'd envisaged for Rob, in terms of education and 'background'; but by the time they realised Rob intended to settle for Emma, she'd won them over and they accepted her unquestioningly. Of course it's from nothing Gran's actually said that I've picked this up. It's just one of those things you know.

It's a calm January night, but I'm shivering in my Darwin clothes when I arrive at Gran's, and get one of her shawls from her cupboard as she makes coffee for us.

'I've decided to find out who Emma was,' I tell her when we're sitting on her little balcony, looking down towards the lights of central Melbourne.

'I thought you might, sooner or later. I knew you were coming close to it when you asked about Emma's things – when was that? Before Christmas sometime.'

'That was when I found out about the cloak. That was the first thing. Then, in Darwin, Kate – I told you about Kate in my letter at Christmas, remember? – Kate thought it was insane that Rob wouldn't talk to me about Emma.'

Gran nodded. 'Yes, it would seem that way to an outsider, I can see that.'

'Well, at first I defended Rob, but then I started to see from Kate's point of view. Emma was becoming less and less real to me and Rob seemed like the villain, keeping all the real memories to himself, shutting me out. And I was just sitting back and letting him, as if I didn't care about her. It was as if – as if – ' I'm grasping around for words.

'I know, dear. Well, did you get Rob to talk?'

'After a battle. I thought I was going to lose everything. But in the end it was good, really. Once he got started, he didn't seem to want to stop. We'd be on site, or driving somewhere, and he'd remember some detail about her. Little things. Like she hated blue cheese. And wanted to learn Spanish. And they were planning to travel overland to England through India after I turned three.'

'You know, I think I remember that crazy plan.'

'Then Kate pushed me on to the next step. She was the one who thought of looking up the 1970s newspapers. Suddenly, there was Emma.' Gran is holding my hands in both of hers. 'I can't leave it there, Gran. I've got to keep going. I want to know every-thing.'

'You know we tried very hard to trace her all those years ago and got nowhere?'

'Yes.' I give her the print from the newspaper. 'Have you got the original, Gran? This one's so blurry.'

'Of course. And other documents from that time as well. It'll take me a while to remember exactly where I've put them, but don't worry, they're here some-where.'

'What sort of things?'

'Oh, clippings from all the papers, autopsy report, coroner's verdict, letters we got in reply to the ads, other photos, dental Xrays, finger-print copy – '

My eyes widen at the list. 'Really? All that?'

'Oh, yes. I tell you, we did a thorough search. Circulated dentists, doctors – '

'Why doctors?'

'Because of the autopsy report. The heart condition she had.'

'What? I didn't know about this!'

'Didn't you? A heart murmur or something. I forget the precise medical term.'

'And this had something to do with her death? Look, Gran, if you don't mind, tell me about it all again. Everything you remember about the drowning.'

'Curiously enough, Ruby, I remember it very clearly. It's the details from last week that tend to elude me. I must be ageing.' The lamplight falls on the 'good' side of her face. Her hair's been recently shaped and tinted, and soft waves frame her face with a fashionable short bob at the back. It's easy to visualise her at the time of Emma's accident. And now just sixteen years later she's lost her husband and her health and she's lucky if she can keep three appointments a week without her strength running out. 'I remember all about that Easter, and the next few weeks. After all, we had to go over and over the story for the police and the newspapers and the people we thought might know something. And then, you've asked me about it, quite frequently, over the years.'

Of course I have. I know the story as well as Gran. Rob and Emma had gone down the coast surfing, leaving me in Melbourne with Gran and Grandpop. Emma had become as mad about surfing as Rob was by this stage. The day it happened, they'd gone right down to Red Beach.

Emma was in the water with her board. Rob was away at the car up near the road getting something and he noticed another car parked up the road a bit. Then he looked out to sea and saw a swimmer thrashing about in the water near Emma. Emma was paddling over, getting close enough to the other swimmer to let him hang onto her board.

Rob started back down to the beach, not in too much hurry because he was quite sure she'd be able to help the swimmer, to tow him on her board to the edge of the rip. Then, the next thing, there was the swimmer body-surfing in to shore alone and collapsing on the sand. But Emma's board was still floating, moving outwards quite quickly with the rip, and there was no sign of Emma.

Rob grabbed his board and rushed straight in. It took him a long time to paddle out against the incoming waves. He found her, her ankle still attached to her board. He tried to resuscitate her there, battling to keep her stable on the board as the rip carried them further from shore. But it was obviously too late.

He managed to paddle her board with her body laid in front of him back through the rip to shore. He tried again to resuscitate her, but it was hopeless.

That is the story. Gran has stopped in her retelling, her face sad.

'The guy she rescued,' I prompt. 'Why didn't he go and get help or an ambulance or something?'

'Well, he simply disappeared. Rob said at one stage he looked for him from out on the water but both the man and his vehicle had gone. Rob thought he'd gone to get help. But he was never seen or heard of again – not by us, anyway.'

'What a criminal.'

'Well, Ruby, he'd feel very bad about it. He'd see it as his fault.'

'It was! It's just the same as a hit-and-run driver.'

'Perhaps not that bad. The autopsy found this heart condition. It's possible that the effort of paddling towards the swimmer, the anxiety, combined with being tumbled off the board by the wave, made her too weak to scramble back on.'

I can't accept that Emma's weak heart made her death any less of a crime. But it's something new, a factor Gran hadn't mentioned before.

Gran and I sit in silence for a while. I'm imagining Rob's anguish and his superhuman effort to save Emma. I've seen that rip at Red Beach.

'But we weren't able to trace a doctor who'd ever treated Emma for her heart murmur. Perhaps she didn't know about it herself,' Gran continues. 'Ah, Ruby, now I remember where I put those papers. I'll fetch them for you.' Some minutes later she brings me a leather case, an old-fashioned Gladstone bag. 'There,' she says. 'Everything's in there.'

'Gran, why haven't you given me these things before?'

'You never asked. And I decided long ago I wouldn't tell you about them unless you did ask. For all I knew you would be content to leave the unknown unknown. I didn't want to be the one to stir you up or make you feel guilty about not wanting to track down your mother's side of the family. And your real father's, too, now I come to think of it. You've been with us so long I tend to forget Rob's not your real father.'

'I wish he were,' I mutter; for suddenly again I feel myself to be a non-person, floating, unanchored. 'Gran, it's so hard to believe that you of all people didn't find out something about her. A name, a school, a town?' Gran knows what I mean. With her acute instinct for where people belong, it's extraordinary she didn't pick up some hint of Emma's background.

'Nothing. Anyway, after a little while I stopped looking. She made Rob happy. Rob's my only child and his happiness is – has always been – the most important thing to me.'

'Emma must have realised that sooner or later I'd need to know about her.'

'Well, my dear, she'd hardly have expected to die so soon. Maybe in time she'd have been able to share her past. She probably thought there was all the time in the world.'

An echo of Rob's words – *I thought we had all the time in the world.* Gran's continuing. 'And don't forget she left you that other name – the name for your friend. Miranda.'

'Did Emma name Miranda? Are you sure?'

'Of course. You knew that.'

I shake my head. Perhaps I did know. I suppose the name had to come from somewhere but I've never wondered where.

'I remember,' Gran is saying, 'it was one day in summer when you were nearly two. I suppose it was not long before the accident. You were in your pushchair, in the shade under a tree and we could hear you chattering just out of our earshot. Emma laughed and said something like don't worry, Ruby's all right, she's just speaking to Miranda. Somehow the name stuck. Until you got a little older, and then you forgot all about Miranda.'

I don't answer. Gran sighs and touches her eyes. She hoists herself from her chair, stoops and kisses my forehead. 'Goodnight, my dear. It's lovely to have you back here. We'll talk again in the morning.'

'Goodnight, Gran.'

The Gladstone bag is heavy. I carry it into the room I'm to sleep in, and snap open the catches at each end. It's full of papers. On top is a large envelope with an undertaker's name on the top left corner. Inside are the photos. There's a letter attached: 'Enclosed are the photographs of the deceased we agreed to supply, those of face and facial profile, and distinguishing bodily marks. The X-rays and fingerprint reproductions will be forthcoming in due course from the appropriate government departments.'

I place the photographs side by side along the bed. There's the photo from the newspapers, and then two profiles labelled left side, right side. Then the same photos, this time in colour, bright and hideous with the lips painted red and the check bones rouged. Still the same closed eyes, crescents of black eyelashes.

Four full-length photos, unclothed: labelled front, back, left side, right side. I gaze at the thin body, sharp hip bones, dark-nippled breasts. I lived for nine months between those hip bones, and fed at those breasts. Emma, who are you?

I'm shivering. Out of my bag from Darwin I unfold Emma's cloak, wrap it around me. I start to wonder if the way it swings is caused by something weightier at the hem than folded fabric. Perhaps I'm thinking of stories of spies and smugglers who conceal their secret documents in the lining of their jackets. With my nail scissors I hack at the stitches holding the lining to the woollen fabric. Cutting and tearing, finally I separate the one from the other, feeling the hems of each carefully then faster and faster in desperation because it's obvious there's nothing hidden in the cloak. Not even a scrap of paper. I finger the lint along the fold inside the woollen hem, and look at the ruins of the beautiful cloak on the bedroom floor. What had I expected to find? A name, address and telephone number? Emma's Medicare card?

It takes me a long time to go to sleep. <u>Emma is suddenly real. For the first time in my life, I grieve for my mother.</u>

## CHAPTER 8

Next afternoon I catch a tram to Fitzroy to see who's home at the house Alex lives in. The street door is standing open. I bang on it but there's no response. I walk up the stairs, calling 'Anyone home?'

The place seems empty without the usual heavy music blaring; most of the doors are closed. The living room is littered with newspapers, abandoned thongs, towels and empty cans. I shift Thomas the cat off the only otherwise empty chair and sit down. I'll wait for a few minutes. Probably they've gone out to buy something.

Gran hadn't been able to add anything this morning. She told me she'd had a restless night, too, going over and over conversations she remembered with Emma for any hint of earlier associations. But of course it was hopeless. She'd gone through that whole process all those years ago.

Together we looked through the twenty or so letters sent in reply to the advertisements. Some were obviously cranky, others next to pornographic. Gran told me they'd followed them up. The police helped, too, particularly with the nasty ones. In most cases it turned out the girl these people thought they recognised was still alive and well. She told me about one distressing case where parents thought it was their daughter, whom they supposed to be on holiday in Greece. I noticed that each of the letters had notes attached with the results of the enquiries. I kept aside the only one they'd been unable to follow up.

The address on it was a YMCA hostel. The writer said he'd seen the girl somewhere and he couldn't remember where but she was one hell of a good waitress. Gran's comment read 'This person was on a hiking holiday and had left the hostel by the time we tried to contact him, and the management had no forwarding address. A young woman still at the hostel had been slightly acquainted with him, and said she heard him say he'd replied to the ad for a joke one night when he was drunk. Electoral roll search etc. did not reveal anyone of his name. Seems pointless to follow this one further.'

I put it aside because of remembering Dave in Darwin talking about Australians working in tourist resort hotels in New Zealand. The New Zealand connection. 'We couldn't start on the process of contacting all the places that employ waitresses,' Gran told me. 'We had to call a stop somewhere. We'd done enough to enable Rob to go ahead with legally adopting you.'

I'm ready to give up waiting at Alex's house when his bedroom door opens and he strolls out, his black hair spiky from sleeping, dressed in his blue robe. He sees me perching in the living room.

'What a surprise,' he drawls. 'Coffee?'

'Okay.'

I follow him across the room to the kitchen and sit on a stool at the bench, watching him push aside dishes in the sink to make room under the tap for the kettle. His chin is stubbled with two days' unshaven growth.

'How was Darwin?'

'The best. Hot and steamy. Brilliant thunderstorms. I met some good people.'

'Yeah?' I notice he's tipping instant coffee into three mugs. No teaspoons around of course. 'I like the haircut.'

'Well, it's easier, in the heat, you know . . .'

'So what did you come back for then?'

'To get some photos and things from Gran. I've decided to try and find out about my mother – ' Just then Alex's bedroom door opens again and a tall model-shaped girl hurries out, hitching a bag over her shoulder with one hand and brushing her hair with the other.

'Alex, it's after one o'clock. I'm going to be hours late for work.'

'This is Ria,' Alex says to me. 'Here's some coffee, Ria.'

'Hi,' I say:

'Haven't got time for coffee. Ring you later, okay?' She drops the hairbrush on the bench, says 'Bye-ee' to me, and we hear her clattering down the stairs.

'Oh, well,' Alex says, pushing one of the mugs of coffee to me, 'I'll drink two then.'

'Didn't take you long,' I say, after a pause.

'You were the one who stuffed off, remember?' he replies immediately.

I shrug, regretting I'd alluded acidly to Ria. It hardly matters, after all.

'What were you saying about your mother? I thought she died when you were a little kid.'

'Yes, but nobody knows who she was, and Rob adopted me – oh, I've told you all this, Alex. So I suppose I'm trying to find out about my mother and my father.'

'God, you're keen. I couldn't wait to get away from mine. So where do you start?'

Suddenly I don't feel like talking to him about it. 'Don't know yet.' The coffee tastes vile. I think the milk's off. 'Where are all the others today, anyway?'

'Who knows? Sandy shifted out last week. I think the others have got jobs just now. Peter's shifting soon. This place is getting a bit of a drag, really.'

'You're thinking of moving?'

'Easier than tidying up. It's getting out of control.'

'Oh, I don't know. Looks the same as usual to me.' At last I get rid of the last bit of coffee. I can't be bothered asking him how his latest money-making project is going, or if he's working at all. 'I might call round later and see the others. They'll be home this evening?'

'Probably. Don't rush off. Stick around while I shower and we'll go down to the cafe or somewhere.'

'No,' I say. 'I've got to see someone.' I make a show of glancing at my watch as I slide off the stool.

'As you like,' he answers casually. 'Might see you later, then.'

'Right.'

I leave the street door downstairs standing open. I'm smiling, almost laughing as I wait at the tram stop. Thank God I got out of that one when I did.

All the same, sitting on the tram trundling towards Victoria Parade, some of the sadness and sense of aloneness I had last night returns and I realise Alex's easy letting go of me has compounded that. We were pretty important to each other once. Can't think why, I tell myself. I keep my eyes wide open and concentrate on the shops and people passing outside so the tears will drain back to where they came from.

The manufacturing jeweller in Collins Street I'd phoned earlier this morning turns the jade earrings over in his hands under his fluorescent tube, a magnifying glass in his left eye. 'Yes, I'd agree,' he says, squinting briefly at me with his right eye. 'New Zealand jade, greenstone. Probably hand carved, and set in decorated sterling silver caps. Not very new. You want to sell these, you said?'

'No, not at all. They belonged to my mother. I wanted to find out where they might have been made, where she would have got them.'

He laughs and the glass drops out of his eye and swings on the end of a string attached to his pullover. 'What am I meant to be – a magician? All I can tell you is that most likely they were originally from New

Zealand. This decoration on the caps – there's nothing unusual about that. It's not hand engraved. It would be made by a punch, something like this.' He picks up a small metal cylinder from his work bench and hands it to me. It's heavy, and tapers to a flat point with a bas-relief surface. 'However, I can say that they're not commercially made, in a factory that is. Look at the back of the caps where they're curved around and soldered. They're not quite the same. A skilful job, and a nice effect. But not what you'd get in a mass-produced line. So you'd be looking for an individual silversmith if you wanted to find the original maker.'

I'm not sure if this is good or bad news. 'Would there be many people doing that sort of work?'

He spread his hands. 'Wouldn't have any idea. Besides, these weren't made recently – '

Over twenty years ago, probably. I suppose I had some notion of going to greenstone-earring sellers and showing them the earrings and Emma's photo. Straight away one of them would say 'Yes, I know her! I sold them to her in December nineteen-something and she worked at thing's down the road and her parents still live around the corner . . .' The utter impossibility of such miracles hits me.

The jeweller sees some of this on my face and speaks kindly. 'I'll give them a polish for you,' he says. 'They're scratched and tarnished. I'll make them look wonderful.'

'No – well, perhaps just one of them. Thank you.'

Looking at me as if I'm stranger than he thought, he hands me back one of the earrings. There's a whirring from the machinery he turns to behind him. 'There,' he says, handing me the earring in a small plastic bag which clicks shut along its top. I look at the glossy green and bright-silver earring through the clear bag and wonder at its sudden newness.

Already the jeweller is busy with something else. 'Thank you,' I say again, and he murmurs 'Have a nice day now' as I leave the shop.

Gran is dozing in the shady corner of the terrace when I arrive. I get juice from the fridge and wander about the apartment. There's a girl from school last year I could phone, in fact should phone I realise with alarm when I recall writing to her from Darwin not so long ago inviting her to come up and stay. I can't be bothered ringing her just then. She'll become like the other school friends I've made over the years. Fading away as I move on to another place. No friends, no – stop feeling sorry for yourself, I say, and shake the ice-cubes in the glass threateningly.

The photos and stacks of letters and documents are neatly arranged on my dressing table. I read the letter from the YMCA again. Terry O'Toole. He wasn't on electoral rolls then, but perhaps that was because he'd been too young to register. But I didn't know how to go about checking electoral rolls. I sit down on the bed. I don't know where to start any of this. I'm not a detective. I don't even like reading detective novels. I consider phoning Rob and telling him I'm calling the whole thing off.

'Ruby? Are you home, dear?'

'Yes, Gran.'

'You should have woken me. I'd have made you a cup of tea.'

'You stay there, Gran – I'll make you one.'

'No,' she says, coming in from the terrace, stretching. 'Sit down for a minute. I've had a thought.' She's looking pleased with herself. 'I remembered a couple who were friendly with Rob and Emma back then. All I could remember was that they were from New Zealand, had come over here to live. So I rang Rob to see if he could remember their names.'

'And did he?'

'Yes – Guy and Jill Turnbull. He thinks they're still living in Sydney.'

'I remember the Turnbulls. They were around sometimes when we lived in Sydney, when I was about twelve.'

'He and Rob were great mates, and so were Emma and Guy's wife Jill. The four of them spent a lot of time together during – during that year. This is what I suggest. You phone them, explain what you're doing. There's just a chance they'll remember something that might help.'

'I don't think I know them well enough to phone them out of the blue. We didn't see them that often in Sydney.' They had a daughter about my age but I didn't get to know her; they lived a distance from us and she went to another school. It seems to me that Rob hasn't ever gone out of his way to see the Turnbulls. Perhaps they remind him of Emma. 'Rob didn't offer to phone them for me, by any chance?'

'No. Actually I suggested that and he wasn't keen to. Perhaps you should give Rob a ring yourself, Ruby. He was sounding just a tiny bit as if you'd abandoned him.'

'What do you mean? Is he angry with me?'

'No, no. Probably he'd like you to let him know yourself how you're getting on.'

'Oh dear, I left in such a rush I hardly noticed how he was taking it. Perhaps he was a bit quiet.' I'm covering up for Gran's sake. Of course I'd noticed that Rob hadn't really agreed to my search for Emma's origins. It was more that he'd given up arguing, withdrawn from the battle. Suddenly I feel very uneasy.

I grab the phone and dial the Darwin number. It's answered almost immediately. It's Evie. It takes her a while to remember who I am, it seems.

'I thought you'd gone back to Sydney, Evie.'

'Did you? Well, I'm back here now. I had some leave owing.'

I asked to speak to Rob. She said he was out for a short time. I asked her to get him to call me as soon as he came in, and hung up. Evie and I never have anything to say to each other.

'Shall I try to talk to the Turnbulls in Sydney, Gran?'

'Why not? The worst they can do is say they hardly remember her at all. But it might get them thinking, and they can phone you back.'

'You and Rob must have talked to them about this when Emma died, surely.'

'Perhaps not all that much. It seems to me it was just before then that they shifted to Sydney, to set up business there. To tell you the truth, I can't now recall if they came back for the funeral. They were what you might call days of turmoil.' Gran closed her eyes for a moment. 'Anyway, we didn't know then about this tenuous New Zealand connection.' She's started using the phrase that keeps coming to my mind. I call Directory and get the Sydney phone number for the Turnbulls.

## CHAPTER 9

T he woman who answers introduces herself as Jill Turnbull. I explain who I am. After a second of silence she says of course she remembers me, and asks after Rob, her voice showing a strong trace of puzzlement.

I tell her why I'm ringing. It comes out incoherently and abruptly and I wish I'd rehearsed it better.

'Of course I remember poor Emma,' Jill Turnbull says slowly. 'But I don't know what we can do to help. We knew her for less than a year. And it was a long time ago.' She pauses. 'I can understand why you're anxious to find out about her, but my dear, she is dead. You still have your father.'

'But Rob's not my father,' I tell her. 'He adopted me after Emma died.'

I hear a slight quick intake of breath, then there's a longer silence. I realise that Jill Turnbull didn't know this, and it's as if the wheels of implication are turning in her head. Finally she says, 'Are you sure, Ruby, that it's a good idea to pursue this search?'

'I'm determined,' I tell her.

'Can I call you back, Ruby? I'll give it some thought. But I'll phone you back anyway, okay? What's the number there?'

I tell her, and hang up, and wait for the phone to ring. Particularly it's Rob's call I'm waiting for. I don't hold out any hope for information from Jill Turnbull.

And anyway this quest of mine is developing an aura of futility, of certain failure. I have nothing to go on, nowhere to start. It's worse now that I have this idea that Rob's suffering. All he has to say to me is come back to Darwin, and I'll be out at the airport like a shot.

So why isn't he returning my call? I'm itching to phone Darwin again, actually reaching for the receiver. And then the phone rings. But it's a local call, no pips announcing a long-distance call. A man's voice asks for Ruby Summerton. It's not Rob. 'Speaking,' I reply without hiding my disappointment.

'I'm sorry – is this a bad time to phone? Shall I call back later? It's Guy Turnbull here. Jill – my wife – asked me to call you.'

'It's all right, I was just expecting someone else. But I don't understand – you're ringing from Melbourne?'

'That's right. We're opening an office in Melbourne, a new branch for the business. These days I'm in Melbourne more than I'm home.'

'I see,' I reply stupidly. The conversation's strange and I feel awkward.

'Anyway, Jill suggested I phone you, and buy you dinner so we can have a chat. The thing is, Ruby, I fly back to Sydney tomorrow, so it'll have to be this evening, or else sometime late next week.'

'Well, okay.' I realise I sound ungracious and after all I was the one who involved the Turnbulls in all this. But what about Rob's phone call? 'This evening, that'd be really nice.' I push enthusiasm into my voice. 'Where and when?'

'What about in an hour or so? Around seven? Ask for me at reception – they'll page me and I'll see you there. There's a nice little bistro here that does a decent steak. I'd like to catch up on what old Rob's been up to.'

I write down the name and address of the hotel and put the receiver down, feeling a reawakening of hope. Even though he probably knows nothing more, it's someone new to talk about Emma with. It takes me a few moments to register the look of doubt on Gran's face. 'I'm wondering, Ruby, if you should be going off into town alone to meet some man at a hotel . . .'

'Oh, Gran. It's Rob's friend and it was your idea to contact them. Come with me then, if you're worried.'

'Not me,' she says. 'It's cold out there tonight.'

It's true. It's one of those summer nights in Melbourne filled with autumn, and I'm still noticing the difference from Darwin temperatures. I wonder what to wear and regret destroying my cloak and stuffing it into the bottom of the wardrobe. My other warm clothes are in Rob's study at the Fitzroy house.

'Gran, I'll have to borrow a jumper or a shawl from you,' I call as I open the wardrobe to see if there's anything warmer than what I've got on. There, falling in folds from a hanger, is my cloak. I take it out slowly and lift the hem. It's been mended, the silk held to the black wool by tiny stitches in a thread exactly matching the gold. I put it on and go out to the sitting room. 'Did you fix this for me, Gran?'

'Well, who else did, do you suppose? The fairies?' I bend down to hug her. 'Such wanton destruction, my girl. It took me hours.'

'I'm sorry – I was looking for – I'd hoped – '

'That's all right, dear. Off you go now and call a cab.'

'And, Gran – I'm expecting Rob to return a call tonight.'

'When he calls I'll explain to him. I'll get him to call later. Don't worry. And good luck.'

There are plenty of people scattered around the velvet chairs and gleaming pillars of the hotel reception area. I hope I'll be able to recognise Guy Turnbull because I know I look very different from when he last saw me. There's a short balding man staring at me; I turn away and study a tank of fish set into the wall.

In the glass side of the tank I see the reflection of the man coming towards me, a strange look on his face. I freeze. I don't want to have to deal with a sleazy pick-up attempt. I hear him say, uncertainly, 'Hello – '

I swing around to face him and see with relief that I recognise him, it's Guy. But he's not smiling and I notice, with surprise, there are tears standing in his eyes.

'You must be Ruby,' he says. I nod. He relaxes a little, puts his hands on my shoulders and gives me a light kiss on the cheek. 'Forgive me – it was seeing you like that which startled me. You looked so much like Emma for a moment, standing there in her cape.'

'I'm sorry. I didn't mean to try and impersonate Emma or anything like that. I know she – wore a cloak similar to – to – ' This is going very badly. I'm starting to stammer. A second bad start: the phone call and now this. My face is reddening and that's not helped by the warmth of the hotel lobby. I slide the cloak off my shoulders. If he notices my embarrassment he doesn't show it and he's recovered his composure.

'The bistro's this way,' he says. 'Come and sit down. I've booked us a little table not too close to the music so we can talk.'

A waiter seats us and whips away my cloak. I ask for a lime and soda when the waiter returns for the drinks order.

'So,' Guy says at last, 'it's not Emma's famous cloak after all. I thought perhaps Rob had kept it all this time. Silly of me. I must have seemed like a man who'd seen a ghost.'

'A little,' I say, and smile, deciding not to tell him that at first I'd taken him for a sleazebag on the make. It looks as if it's going to be a difficult enough evening as it is. I feel uncomfortable, sure that this is all a mistake. Why would the Turnbulls remember anything? Guy doesn't even look the type who'd care. After all, there's no money in it for him.

But it's not so bad. We talk about Rob and what he's been doing. Because I'm so familiar with Rob's work it's easy for me to chatter on knowledgeably and Guy's impressed or says he is anyway. He tells me his business is diversifying into motel construction, and that it's about time he and Rob got together on a project again. He asks if Rob's ever remarried.

'Lots of girlfriends,' I tell him, 'but no wife.'

'I'm not surprised. I remember when that harridan from the orchestra – the violin player or whatever she was – was doing her damnedest to get him to the altar. Remember her? Rob told me then one night when we'd had a few that he had no intention of marrying again.'

Our dinners have been delivered: steak for him, fish for me. I store the information that Guy thinks Emma and Rob were married – or perhaps he's putting it that way out of some attempt to spare my feelings – and say, 'I don't recall the violinist as being the marrying and settling down type.' I wonder how to push the talk on to Emma.

'Rob says you and Jill were originally from New Zealand.' He nods, not looking up from the slab of steak he's slicing. I get the earrings out of my pocket and put them on the table near his glass of red wine. 'Gran gave me these. They were among Emma's things.' They lie on the white tablecloth.

'Greenstone,' he says briefly.

I don't wait to explain why one is shiny and the other not, and hurry on, 'You and Jill didn't know that Rob's not my natural father?'

'That's right. We didn't.'

'So you didn't know Rob before he met Emma?'

'No – we met them both shortly after we arrived from New Zealand. Through work, initially. But Emma and Jill were around the same age and both had little kids – Rob and Emma were our first and closest friends in Melbourne. But we only stayed ten months or less. Went on over to Sydney.' He smiles. 'It seems strange now, looking back, that we all spent so much time together and yet obviously knew so little about each other. Backgrounds, I mean. At that age, in those days anyway, you took people how you found them. Current issues, current music, future plans; things like that were the talk, I guess.'

I feel he's leading away from direct talk about Emma. 'I want to find out who she was,' I say, 'and, of course, who my real father was or is.'

Guy speaks slowly. 'If Emma went to so much trouble to hide her identity, don't you think you might be opening up a can of worms?'

'I don't care. I can take it. What I can't take is not knowing. But I don't know where to start.'

He placed his hands palms down on the table rather as if at last he would open a book and let me read. 'When Jill rang earlier this evening she was very concerned about what you were trying to do – for your sake, you understand. This can-of-worms stuff. Because she'd realised that if Rob wasn't your father then the mystery was so much deeper. She said I should take you out for a meal, try to talk you out of doing it.' He looks at me steadily. 'The plan was also to check you out. See if you were just a hysterical kid.' I take a deep breath, my eyes fixed on his. 'If not, I should tell you what we know. Don't get your hopes up,' he goes on quickly, 'it's not much. And Jill told me something else she hadn't before.'

'What?'

'Hang on, hang on, let me tell it my way. When we first met Rob and Emma, we thought at once she was a New Zealander. But when we mentioned it at some stage quite early in the friendship, she denied it and laughed it off in that charming way she had and turned the conversation into a game of swapping anti-New Zealand and anti-Aussie jokes, you know the kind of thing. But Jill and I were still puzzled, and discussed it between ourselves, because of the distinctive vowel sounds in her accent. But I just thought, if I thought much more about it at all, that she'd picked it up from us or some other Kiwis and was mimicking us now and then to send us up.

'However, it seems Jill wasn't convinced. Apparently one night when Rob and I were off somewhere and Emma and Jill were having a girls' session – probably over a flagon of rough red and a few joints, knowing them – Jill questioned her again. Yes, said Emma, she was a Kiwi, but she didn't want to say any more and she begged Jill never to give anyone even that little clue about her background, whatever happened. And Jill never did. Until she told me tonight.'

So much to take in, and yet in a way not surprising. 'But why – I mean if she was a New Zealander – didn't they trace her through her passport? I know the police checked that sort of thing . . .' My voice trails off. I've already considered the possibility that Emma Blake wasn't her real name.

'That's just the thing, Ruby. Those days you didn't need a passport to travel between Australia and New Zealand. I don't know how widely the search was conducted in New Zealand, if at all. That's something you'll have to find out. But you'll have to realise, that if the photographs were circulated in New Zealand and there were no takers, it means people didn't want to know.'

'I've already thought about that,' I reply in a dull voice. 'I mean, it applied if she'd been an Australian, didn't it? But, anyway, I don't think there was much advertising done in New Zealand. I don't think anyone considered a New Zealand connection.'

'So, Ruby, what now?'

'I'm not sure. I think I'd like to go home, Guy, and think about all this.'

'Of course.' He signals a waiter and asks him to call a taxi. 'Are you all right? Would you like me to come with you in the cab?'

'No, no, I'm fine.' I smile at him. 'Really.' He holds up the cloak and as I wriggle my shoulders into it and gather it around me, I say, 'Actually, I'm sure this is Emma's cloak. I found it in a second-hand shop. Both Rob and Gran recognised it.'

'What a perfect coincidence.' He escorts me to the taxi, and kisses me again on the cheek. 'The very best of luck, Ruby. Phone us any time you need any help – we probably don't have any more information for you but we might think of some angles you won't. And let us know how you get on, won't you?'

Guy Turnbull has changed Emma for me again, given her a new dimension. She's no longer Australian as we'd all taken for granted. I remember the tears in his eyes when he'd first seen me, surprising tears when I think of the sort of man he appears to be. I had reminded him of Emma. She still has this strong effect on people.

It's colder. I'm shivering in the taxi and huddle into the cloak. The sense of aloneness creeps around me again, and I long for the taxi to hurry me to Gran's and her news of Rob's phone call.

## CHAPTER 10

'Did he phone?'

Gran's watching television and working on a crossword puzzle. She shakes her head.

'No, he didn't. Why not call him now?'

I hold the phone while it rings and rings and nobody picks it up at the other end. I replace the receiver and shrug. 'They must have all gone out tonight.'

'Phone him later, or in the morning,' Gran says.

'Maybe.' I drop the cloak over the back of the chair near hers.

'Pour me a small port, will you, Ruby?' I pour one for myself too, and take them to the low table between the big chairs. 'Well, what happened? What's he like these days?'

'I didn't like him much at first. He was sort of affable and distant uncle-ish if you know what I mean. Then there was lots of big-boys' talk about property consortiums and company diversification and multi-million rip-off development on the Gold Coast. I started to realise why Rob hadn't bothered to keep in contact with him over the past years. Then I had to push him to the subject of Emma and he softened a bit. I thought perhaps he might have been okay before he grew up to be a tycoon.'

'My memory of those two is that they came over here to make a quid, flower children or not.'

'Well, it seems they made it. Anyway, he didn't have anything I didn't know to tell me – at first.'

'At first?'

'Suddenly he dropped all this condescending stuff and started talking to me like one human being to another.' I tell Gran, as much word for word as I can remember it. She listens without interrupting, and then sits quietly for some time.

'There could be unhappiness at the end of this project, Ruby,' she says at last.

'Things that were considered horrendous twenty years ago aren't necessarily so bad these days, Gran.'

'What are you going to tell Rob?'

'I'm not sure.' I'm suddenly so overwhelmed by tiredness I can't think it out clearly. If I tell him the Turnbulls knew she was a New Zealander, won't he think it's odd they didn't say so years before? And I'm not sure I want to tell him about Emma's strange injunction on Jill to keep silent.

'Sleep on it,' Gran says as if she's reading my thoughts. 'It'll seem clearer in the morning.'

*I'm on a bus full of people, sitting right up there close to the driver. It's dark, and the headlights flash over thorns leaning across the roadway as we race past. We career into tunnels where people press back to get out of our way and yet it seems to me that they're grasping out as if to claw us from the bus. There's a pain, low in my stomach, which starts to glow with the redness of an ember, and I clutch my hands over it because I know the speed we're moving will fan it into a flame and then a raging fire. At the end of the last tunnel we plunge downwards through rocks, the bus rocking violently as it follows no road at all but fights to stay upright. I'm thrown about and I should be gripping the seat to protect myself but I can't; I have to keep my hands clenched over this growing ember in my stomach. Already its redness shines through my hands and they're glowing and reflecting off the glass and chrome around me at the front of the bus.*

I'm aware somehow that I'm dreaming and try to wake. But it's as if I have no will of my own, and I'm drawn on into the dream.

*Ahead there's a smooth valley floor, a circle of people in black and white from the darkness of the night and the piercing headlights of the bus, which slows, and the people nearest draw back to make a gap in the circle, and in the centre there's something black, and deep. The circle closes behind the bus and people reach in to pull me out. They're grabbing my arms pulling me towards the black pit – don't, please don't, I plead but it's too late – and the flames leap out from the ember, dart after dart of fire which fasten to the crowding people who now reel back, shrieking as they're covered with red flames and I scream –*

I'm awake again. I lie wondering if the scream in my nightmare is still echoing around the bedroom, if I have actually screamed aloud in my sleep and woken Gran. But the apartment is silent, and as minutes pass I breathe more easily, knowing she hasn't been disturbed. Now I can't recall much of the dream. It's dissolving as I think back. There're black and white shapes and redness; and overwhelmingly a sense of powerlessness. The bed's untidy and feels clammy.

I switch on the light and remake the bed, slowly, methodically, consciously calming myself so I'll be able to go back to sleep. Again in bed, I try a meditation technique. I'm lying on my back on a lilo, gently floating in a small swimming pool; there's a breeze and warm sunshine. I have a shady hat over my face, and I can hear birds singing, delicate chimes and soft swishes of leaves.

*I'm lying face downwards on a small raft, gently floating in a small swimming pool; there's a breeze and the salty smell of the sea. Gulls are calling. I let my arms slip off each side of the raft and trail in the water. So restful. Gentle hands seem to caress my fingers as I drift past.*

*The hands become stronger, more grasping. Suddenly my hands are gripped and I know the raft's being pulled to the dangerous open sea as it starts to rock violently in the growing waves. Spray stings my face. Wildly I look ahead and there's that circle of people, drained of colour in the harsh sunshine, gathered waiting for me around the black pit –* 'Miranda!' I shout. 'Help me, Miranda!'

*At once the gripping hands soften and hold mine gently, stroking my fingers. The waves subside. Peace.*

'Ruby, Ruby, are you all right?' I open my eyes and see the light's on and the anxious voice is Gran's. I'm on my stomach, half out of bed and again the sheets and bedspread are in disorder and sweaty.

'Just a nightmare, Gran,' I say groggily, sitting up on the edge of the bed and pressing my fingers on my eyes. 'I'm sorry, did I call out and wake you?'

'It's all right. I was awake. But you did call out.' She sits beside me on the bed, stroking my hair. 'You were shouting to Miranda and I came in because it sounded as if you were in distress.'

'Just a nightmare,' I repeat. 'Did I really call out for Miranda?' I'm not sure now if it was a nightmare. I remember being afraid, but didn't the danger recede?

Gran is speaking again, rocking me gently. 'I'm getting up now, I always do at this time. I like to drink my tea and watch the dawn come over the city. Why don't you crawl into my bed and sleep some more? It's warm and soft and you'll sleep restfully there.'

I let her lead me through to her room, and I'm asleep even as she closes the door.

It should have been a day of action but now it's dark again. I've done nothing all day but mope about Gran's apartment. I woke in her wide fluffy bed and wouldn't get up for two hours and only did then because sunshine filled the room and it was hot. I'm weighed down all day by the almost forgotten bad dreams of the previous night, the information about Emma from Guy Turn-bull, the recognition that what I want so desperately is going to require a superhuman effort. (And why did I call out to Miranda in the middle of a nightmare?)

Some time during the day Gran went out and started an enquiry to search the electoral rolls for Terry O'Toole, the man who'd seen Emma as a waitress somewhere. When she came back I asked her why she had this reputation for being vague, because it seems to me she's quite the opposite.

She replied, inconsequentially, that she knew someone who knew someone who had the connections to find these things out and anyway these days all they had to do was press a button on a computer and they could search the rolls in twenty-five seconds. Anyway, an hour or so later they phoned and gave us the address of fourteen Terence O'Tooles all over Australia, and this adds to the weight, the weight of difficulty.

I miss Rob dreadfully. I've phoned the Darwin house seven times, but there's never any reply.

## CHAPTER 11

And then, the eighth time I try the Darwin number, there's Rob on the other end. By this time I'm in such a state from not being able to get him all those other times I can hardly speak coherently. 'Why didn't you phone me back?' I end up saying.

'Was I supposed to phone you, Ruby? I'm terribly sorry, I didn't know. Was it something important?'

He didn't get the message to phone me. Evie forgot to tell him. It was as simple as that.

'I just wanted to tell you how I was getting on.' In my relief to be in contact with Rob again I talk on for several moments – about seeing Guy Turnbull, about the development of the New Zealand connection, even about what a yawn Alex turned out to be – before I realise something's still wrong. There's a coolness coming over the phone to me and it matches the cold feeling inside I've had every time I've thought of Rob recently.

'Rob, are you sure – um – you don't mind that I'm going off to find out about Emma?'

Instantly he replies, 'How could I mind? She was your mother, Ruby, and you must follow it through if that's what you want.'

'Well . . . that's okay, then.'

But it's not okay, I know, and after we finish the awful polite conversation I know it's done me no good. The cold feeling's still there inside. Rob was distanced from me by more than the thousands of kilometres between here and Darwin. He's never been like that before. It's very different from the 'Come back to Darwin!' that I'd expected.

So my gloom deepens. I drag myself around Gran's apartment. Going back to my old life is now as hard as going on to new things. I don't know what to do. I'm limp with indecision. I'm starting to see that with Rob around I've never had to make any moves on my own. Always he's been the motivator, the front that's given me an aura of being a free and independent spirit. But I'm not. On my own I'm hopeless.

How do you make decisions? People talk about thinking the options through, weighing the pros and cons. I can't see things so clearly. There's only a confused muddle of half-thought-out desires and beyond that a great unknown.

Gran's worried about me. 'I finally talked to Rob,' I tell her, 'and he was sort of, well, funny. I think he's washed his hands of me.'

'Of course he hasn't. He's just finding out what it's like to be a parent when the child finds its wings and starts to fly solo.' She's trying to comfort me, and she is, a little. Then she says, 'I wish he'd get around to finding himself a mate. He should have married years before. If only he'd fall in love.'

'He does. Often. They just don't last very long.'

'Poor Ruby,' she says, and brings me coffee. I pretend to read a book and close my eyes and long to be twelve again with Miranda as my ally.

There was a time years ago at a strange wild place, a raw new town hacked into the hillsides, the red earth tumbling into the valley from hasty foundations, a gaping hole where the ground trembled with machinery chewing at it. It was a gold-mining camp. I don't remember why Rob was there. We weren't there for long, not long enough for us to find a proper place to live or for me to go to school.

Anyway there was no school there. There were no children my age. There was nothing to do. I suppose I should have been bored but looking back I have no memory of time dragging. Of course there was Miranda. But also at that time I had a life rich in fantasy. I was inventing stories that in the span of a day grew into long plays in which I played every part. Maybe it was the constant rumble of heavy machinery ripping into the earth that triggered the subject of my plays. They were epics with backgrounds of wars or earthquakes or burning cities. The earthmoving machinery provided the soundtrack of rumbling tanks, the whine of attacking jets, the roar of a ravening fire, the sickening crashes of collapsing buildings.

In my plays I was both victim and heroic rescuer. The war play was the best. It went through many rehearsals and refinements. I was the gunner trapped in a burning tank in the centre of a minefield. I was the brave soldier picking my way over the minefield, dodging exploding mines and volleys of machine-gun fire on my way to rescue the gunner.

Miranda never joined in the playmaking. She would have been useful. She didn't refuse, exactly; she was absent. The plays took shape in the backyard of the block of temporary housing where Rob and I were staying along with other people involved with the mining project. It wasn't much of a backyard, just an extension of the area that had been roughly flattened to make space for the housing block. But it was excellent for a minefield or an earthquake.

The plays stopped when Miranda let me know that Mrs Bee, the camp cook and housekeeper, had been telling her drinking mates that the architect's daughter was touched in the head. She said I shouted and argued with people who weren't there, ran about dodging things which weren't moving. I had no idea she or anyone else had been watching. I was deeply embarrassed. I knew I'd now be too self-conscious to ever try any more storymaking. I dreaded seeing Mrs Bee and started off for a long walk along the rough road away from the mining camp.

I remember Rob's warning not to go far from the camp. But I knew there was only one road to the camp, and I was on it. How could I get lost?

It was winter. The sunlight was strong but not very hot. The sun hung low in the sky, and as the bush thickened further from the camp black shadows crouched at the side of the road. The noise of the machinery faded, and the silence seemed to gather around me. These are the first things I remember from that walk: the harsh sunlight and the inky shadows, and the silence growing like a surrounding presence. I scuffed my feet to disturb the quietness and the red dust of the road swirled and hung in the still air. A bird shrieked once, quite close, startlingly; and as that sound receded I realised there was no longer any trace of noise from the earthmovers at the camp.

It was about then that I thought someone was following me. There seemed to be an echo of my footsteps, but when I stopped that echo stopped too. And when I turned quickly, it seemed the shadows at the edge of the road moved quickly before the stillness and silence closed in again.

*Who is it, Miranda? Can you see anyone?* She couldn't, or at least she didn't answer.

I was thirsty and very tired. I wanted to go back to the camp, but I was certain there was something following me. Turning back might bring me face to face.

Then I knew. The footsteps broke into a run and as I whirled around I saw a figure dash from the road among the trees and scrub. I was staring into the sunlight. Something was in the bush, running fast, drawing level with me. The strong light and black shadows tricked my eyes and while I could follow the flickering of light and darkness I couldn't fix on the mover.

*Now's the time to run*, my brain told me but I couldn't move. Suddenly the movement in the bush stopped and there was a simultaneous shout of pain.

Silence again, then a groan. The shadows were still. There was no more movement.

I spoke to Miranda. *Go home*, she said.

Far more real, it seemed to me, was the voice in the bush whimpering for help.

In the years since, I've pushed the memory so deep I can't remember now what the man looked like. I was eleven years old and knew about avoiding situations with strangers. I had to balance against that the calls for help.

He was sprawled on the ground. His left leg was twisted behind him. It was caught in the fork of a fallen branch.

'Help me shift that branch,' he groaned.

I circled around, keeping my eyes on him. He roared with pain when I dragged at the branch and it shifted suddenly with a lurch, releasing his ankle. I stood horror stricken as he writhed and moaned.

'You'll have to help me get back to my house,' he said at last, his voice distorted by his clenched teeth.

'Where?

He raised his arm and flapped his hand weakly in a direction deeper into the bush. I didn't move. 'Come on!' he demanded more strongly. 'There's a phone there – can't you see I need a doctor?' He stretched his arm towards me. 'Please? Won't you help me up?'

Unwillingly I stepped towards him. His eyes had a

pitiful pleading look in them. He held my arm. He had a sickening smell.

At that instant some sense told me that I'd never be strong enough to haul such a big man to his feet and anyway that wasn't what he had in mind. He saw this realisation on my face. In the same instant his grip tightened and his eyes changed. I felt myself losing balance.

He was too late. An amazing burst of strength helped me wrench free in time. I ran.

I heard him cursing and crashing through the undergrowth after me. But there, suddenly, was the red dust of the road and I could run faster. I ran until there was no sound of him. There were only my gasping sobs. I ran until my legs were too weak to hold me up. I collapsed on the road. At last I could breathe properly again, my heart stopped leaping. Once more the silence closed in.

I had run a long way. I should have been close to the mining camp, but I couldn't hear the machinery. The road stretched into the hazy distance exactly the same in both directions. In my panic I'd burst from the bush onto the road and run in the direction I'd been walking. That is, further away from the camp.

I cradled my head and rocked in despair. How could I walk back along that road? The man might be hiding in wait for me. The shadows thickened. It wouldn't be light for much longer. I stood and turned around and around trying to see where the sun was, until I realised I could no longer remember which direction the camp was.

In the distance, as far as I could see along the road, was a smudge of dust. It was growing. Then I saw it was a landrover racing towards me. I didn't know whether to hide or wave my arms for help. I quivered with indecision and did neither. The landrover screeched and stopped. As the dust settled I saw Rob's horrified face.

'Ruby!' he shouted, leaping out. I was crying and shaking with relief and exhaustion. He lifted me into the landrover and cuddled me until I calmed down. Then he drove me back to the mining camp.

Some time later, after all the fuss had died down, I asked Miranda why she'd left me alone on that road. I remember her reply: didn't I realise she'd sent Rob to find me? And, at the time, when she said that, I believed her.

It seems to me now, sitting here on Gran's terrace in my black mood, Miranda would have been more helpful if she'd sent Rob to find me a lot sooner. And what's more I'm not even allowed to continue this luxury of gloom in solitude. Gran's calling me to the telephone. The phone's ruling my life these days.

It's Kate. It's a relief to talk to her but it takes me a minute to grasp what she's saying.

'I'm taking leave, Ruby, two months' holiday, two whole months so I can come to New Zealand with you! Isn't it great?'

'I don't understand. I mean, it's great news, but – how come?'

'We get troppo leave every now and then, so I thought why not go to New Zealand with you and help you look for Emma. You know, two people can travel cheaper together, and two heads are better than one – '

'Hang on, Kate, are you sure you want to use up your precious leave to come to New Zealand on what might be a boring waste of time? And can you afford it?' I'm wondering if this was all Rob's idea. Perhaps he's paying for Kate to come with me. Perhaps he's relented, decided to give me support in this round-about way.

'Of course I do. I mean it'll be a new country for me, won't it? And I'll have enough money. Evie's given me some. She's got heaps anyway. She made my air bookings, paid for the tickets.'

'Evie did?'

'And it'll be cool weather for a change. We're supposed to go somewhere cool on troppo leave. In fact I'll probably freeze. When I get to Melbourne, Ruby, you'll have to come with me to buy woollies and thermal underwear.'

She's arriving in Melbourne the day after tomorrow, and two days later we're to fly to Auckland. She tells me her flight number, tells me to phone immediately to book on the same flight.

I tell Gran that we're going to have Kate to stay for a couple of nights and that then, at last, I'll be making a move. Going to New Zealand.

'Good,' she said briskly. She reminds me to get copies made of one of the photos of Emma; and that gives me something to do to fill in the rest of the day.

I guess Gran will be glad to see the back of me in my present mood.

I've been in Melbourne ten days now. HSC results are due any day. Higher School Certificate, that final school exam, the so-called ticket to my future.

In the evening Jill Turnbull phones from Sydney. She asks if I'm going ahead with my search for Emma's origins. I tell her that it looks as if I am.

'That's good, Ruby. Well, look, I wanted to reassure you about what Emma said to me – I mean, I'm sure it's not as if she was a murderer or something or ran away from jail.' She laughs a little and goes on. 'Remember how young we were, Ruby, only a year or so older than you are now, really. And we were sixties kids, you know, hippies, caught up in mysticism and fatalism and love and flowers. Emma especially was fascinated by spiritualism. I mean she believed in a whole tangle of theories of reincarnation and life after death, ghosts, voices from the grave, all that stuff.'

'I'm not sure what you're telling me.'

'I'm not sure, either. Ruby, look, I think it's mainly this. Remember how young we were. I mean that secrecy she swore me to might have been just some dramatic stand that we'd have laughed over a couple of years later. I've been thinking about it in the last day or two and I had to ring and say please don't be put off by what I told Guy to pass on to you. I think it's a great thing you're doing, and I really understand why you have to, and, well, I guess, just good luck. I wish you the very best of luck.'

## CHAPTER 12

W e're in New Zealand, heading for the place called Waitomo Caves.

It's not hard to find. There are tourist brochures at Auckland airport in the lounge where we wait for our rental car. 'Set in dramatic sandstone formations, the underground jewels glitter . . .'

I had scarcely been aware during those last days in Melbourne that Gran had started phoning the list of Terence O'Tooles supplied by the electoral office. It had been a grim job for her. Each call needed explanations leading to the unlikely question – were you staying at a YMCA in Sydney sixteen years ago?

The ninth Terence O'Toole thought he had. He listened as Gran explained about the photograph in the newspaper, the reply sent by someone with his name. After a silence, the man said he guessed he did recall something about that. Gran told me later how she'd crossed the fingers on one hand and gripped the receiver very tightly with the other as she asked him if his reply had been a joke.

'Dear me,' Gran said, 'he sounded scandalised at the suggestion. He said he wouldn't have dreamed of making a joke about such a serious matter. He's probably a respectable insurance salesman and father of five by now. He disowns his disorderly youth.' He couldn't remember where he'd seen the woman whose photo was in the advertisement, but he was sure it was in New Zealand somewhere. He agreed to look at a map and see if any of the place-names rang a bell. Waitomo was the place he recalled. He thought he'd been there in the summer of 1967.

And then Kate arrived in Melbourne, multi-coloured curls and golden skin, shivering and complaining about the weather as I knew she would. It was good to see her. She bought jeans and jumpers in a whirlwind shopping trip and suddenly here we are, on the other side of the Tasman Sea, in another country.

Well, I suppose it was what I was asking for: a jolt out of my apathy and indecision, a push in some direction, any direction, as long as it's movement.

And now that I am moving, I want to get straight to the only place-name we have as a clue. I don't want to waste time on the sights of Auckland. Kate grumbles, but only mildly. As soon as we get our rental car, we drive south.

It's a windy summer's day with a touch of winter hidden in the sudden squalls of rain. In the periods of bright sunshine there's the wet-earth smell I noticed when we first left the airport. The greenness of the farmland seems to glow. Mostly, however, we keep our eyes on the road and drive purposefully. I'm driving while Kate follows with her finger the scheme of the road on the map. We're not here to be tourists, we're thinking, I suppose.

Late afternoon we have coffee and toasted sandwiches at a roadhouse by the river. Across the slow deep water of the Waikato River there's a massive powerhouse. The woman who serves us doesn't know how long it will take to get to Waitomo and doesn't want to find out for us. She admits grudgingly that it will be dark in an hour or two.

'Perhaps we should book into a motel for the night,' Kate says.

I shake my head. I *have* to get to Waitomo. Even this stop seems a waste of time.

'Look,' Kate goes on, 'we had a really early start this morning.' She stabs her finger at the open map on the table. 'It'll be dark soon. Look how winding that road is. There's nothing for miles. What say we get lost? Run out of petrol?'

'We'll be all right,' I reply stubbornly. Kate looks annoyed. For a moment I think she's going to pull age on me. But then she's lived all her life in one town. Going to strange places doesn't worry me, even in the dark. We have a map and a reliable car.

At that moment the rain barrels down again so heavily that the powerhouse disappears in the gloom. Kate's annoyed look remains. All the signs are bad. For the first time I wonder if travelling with Kate will go as smoothly as I'd assumed.

As I was realising that it hadn't even been my choice

to come here with Kate – it was all somehow decided for me – she says, 'Well, if we're going, let's go.'

'At least let's wait until the rain stops.'

'No, you want to go on, let's go now.'

Reluctantly I let her take over the driving. I decide that if she turns off the road into a motel and refuses to go any further, I'll have to give in.

It's dark by the time we leave the main road and head west, following the sign to Waitomo Caves. We've hardly spoken all this way. Kate's driving as if she's on the open road from Darwin to Katherine but I don't dare try to slow her down after a look at her determined face.

The road narrows and starts to wind. At last Kate is forced to lift her foot a little from the accelerator. And then, we're there. A well-lit white wooden hotel. This is it.

Kate drives in to the carpark. She stops the car, then leans across and gives me a quick shoulder hug. 'Okay, you win. We made it.' She's smiling. Tension flies away.

We're here. I don't know what I expected. What happens is that we check in to a unit, lie on our beds with a cup of coffee and the TV on, and I fall asleep almost immediately.

The next morning I take my photo of Emma and ask to speak to the manager. 'It's like this,' he tells me. 'For a start, I'm a relieving manager. I've only been here four weeks myself. If she worked here as a holiday job twenty years ago we wouldn't have any records now. I mean, we're only required to keep tax records for seven years anyway, and you must realise the staff turnover – young people working here for a few weeks over the summer season then moving on – '

Kate and I wander along the road a little. The day's warm, late summer again. 'You shouldn't have had such high hopes,' she murmurs. It's not much of a comfort.

Later she says, 'We shouldn't give up, shouldn't lose hope. You'll see, Ruby, you'll find out one thing, then another and then everything'll happen at once. It always goes like that.'

Mid-morning brings tourist buses.

'We might as well see the caves while we're here,' Kate says.

'Not today.'

'How long do you want to stay?'

'I don't know.'

'My funds aren't endless,' Kate says after a while. 'It's not cheap here. And how long are we going to keep the car?'

'The car's my expense,' I say firmly. Rob's expense, anyway, I say to myself. 'Why don't we see if we can get jobs here?'

We agree that's a good idea. But I persuade her to put off asking about jobs until the next day. In the afternoon we visit the caves.

We're in the dark, obeying the instructions to be silent. The boat moves without a sound on the black water. Suddenly millions of stars appear. We're moving through the galaxy. They're glow-worms hanging perhaps at arm's length and then stretching upwards into the blackness at heights I can't guess, merging into a blur of light. The stars are mirrored in the water. I'm going into the centre of the earth but the images in my mind are of going outwards into space.

By the next morning Kate is determined to check out. When I wake she's packed and ready to go.

'I don't want to go yet.'

'Look, Ruby, this is obviously a dead end. We've asked everybody here, we've asked at the local store and the museum shop, and nobody recognises the photo or can even suggest anyone who might have been around here twenty years ago. We'd get much further going back to Auckland and trying to trace her through the police or something – some welfare organisation or the Salvation Army. They might advise us of the best way to advertise, for instance.'

'I don't want to involve the police. Not yet.'

'And I can't afford to stay on here. My money'll only go so far, you know. This is hardly the cheapest place in New Zealand.'

'We'll try to get jobs here,' I say.

There are no jobs here. 'The main season's over,' the manager says, a trace impatiently. We've changed from paying customers into kids looking for a job.

Kate's keen to get back to Auckland, I know. I want to delay that a little longer. 'Do you know of any other jobs around here?'

He thinks, frowning, tapping his careful fingernails on the reception desk. 'Tell you what,' he says at last. 'When you get back to the main road, head north to

Ohaupo. I've got a mate running a motel just past there. It's called Avalon Inn. His wife's about to have another infant. They might need a hand for a few weeks.' He stopped our thank yous. 'Mind you it'll be work in exchange for accommodation. Don't go pulling any union stuff on them.'

I sense Kate's mood and get in first. 'Could you ring your friend and say we're coming? Put in a good word for us?'

The Avalon is light years away from our last stop. There are eight units facing each other in two rows of four, painted a long time ago in a turquoise paint now faded in patches to chalky blue. There's a carpark in front of each unit's door. There are no cars except for a lopsided Holden stationwagon at the side of a little building at the end of the two rows. We drive towards that building, following the arrow marked Reception.

We press a bell and a woman comes out, plodding, heavily pregnant. 'You're the girls Rob rang about,' she says flatly. My mind reels. Rob? But of course she means the man from the hotel at Waitomo. His name must be Rob as well. I realise this but it's too late. I'm washed with homesickness and longing to see Rob again. I want my old life back.

Kate's dealing with everything. She's negotiating accommodation with a maximum number of hours' work in return. She bargains for a rate per hour above that. The woman agrees and in the background the wail of a baby mounts. There's the whine of a child cut short by a man's snarl.

In a kind of a dream I follow Kate back to the car. She turns it around and parks it outside one of the units nearest the road.

'She probably thinks this glossy latest model will be a come-on for passing trade,' I hear Kate say as we unlock the door to the unit. 'Which reminds me, Ruby, we'll have to return this car! It's too expensive to keep any longer.'

'I think I'll phone Rob,' I tell her. It's not the sort of motel that has a phone in every unit.

We go back to reception. Kate says, 'Ruby has to make a reverse-charge call to Australia.'

'You mean a collect call?' the woman asks doubtfully. But she points to the phone. I let Kate place the call. After all, I realise, it's her house we're ringing.

When Rob's on the line, she hands the phone to me. 'We've got a job for a little while,' I tell him. It's a feeble thing to be saying, given what I'm feeling to be talking to him again, this sense of longing to be back on the old easy footing with Rob.

'Great,' I hear. 'What's the phone number there?'

I tell him, reading it from the disc in the centre of the round dial. 'But, Rob, Waitomo didn't work. I didn't find out anything about Emma.'

There's a silence. 'Rob?'

'I'm sorry to hear that, Ruby-baby. But listen, what about those amazing HSC results? I was so proud of you. Great marks. The world's yours.'

'Rob. You're exaggerating.' The truth is that when the results of the exams had arrived through the post, those exams that had dominated most of my life

116

through 1986, they seemed almost irrelevant, like an obsession of an earlier life. I was too fired up over Kate's arrival and our imminent departure on my quest. I'd given the piece of paper to Gran and asked her to send it on to Rob.

Rob's speaking again. 'And I've got some good news of my own. I hope you'll be pleased.' He's speaking quickly, as if to get it out before I interrupt. 'It's Evie. You remember the gorgeous Evie? We're going to get married. She's agreed. She's going to marry me as soon as possible.'

Perhaps I'm imagining that his voice sounds cold and triumphant.

'Ruby? Are you still there?'

I want to die.

## CHAPTER 13

'**Y**ou were an utter bitch on the phone, Ruby.' My face is buried in the thin candlewick bedspread. 'Ruby? What's going on? You were hanging out to talk to Rob. Next thing you're hanging up on him. Ruby? Are you going to talk?' I hear the car keys jingle. 'Well. I'm going to find a store and get some things.'

The motel unit is furnished in brown and lime green. The bedspreads are faded orange. My old life with Rob seems very far away. It looks like it's gone for ever.

I thought we'd last here two days, three at the most. But Kate takes to this job as if it were made for her. She's competent and a good organiser. By the end of the first week it's as if she's the manager. The Frasers, the couple who own the motel, retreat into their domestic turmoil and leave her to it.

I'm just the chambermaid. It suits me. Every morning I clean the units that were occupied the night before. I'm engulfed in misery. Perhaps 1987 will be the worst year of my life. Anyway it seems right to be spending every morning dumping into black plastic rubbish bags the chaos of other people's night-before. I have to count the knives and forks and glasses and pillows to see how many have been nicked. It's a dodgy sort of guest we get here sometimes.

Each unit is reborn into sparkling order when I leave it. I know next morning it will be a mess again. It's just like life.

Kate helps me sometimes. Other times she's on the phone at reception, organising things, taking bookings. I heard her shouting at the laundry company for not ironing the sheets properly. She walks about purpose-fully and her eyes sparkle. She's in heaven.

We don't ever discuss my phone call to Rob. He doesn't ring me back.

'There's a band playing at the local pub tonight,' Kate says. 'Why don't we go?'

'Sounds awful.'

'It probably will be awful but it's Friday night and we've been sitting here night after night for over a week now, and you're getting more and more depressed.' Kate looks into my face earnestly. 'I know that looking for Emma doesn't seem to be getting anywhere but it doesn't hurt to have a bit of a rest for a while. We knew it wasn't going to happen all at once, didn't we?'

At least she's stopped urging me to go to the police.

'Is it really Friday today?'

'Of course it is, you twit. Come on. We'll eat at the pub. We don't have to stay long if it's impossible.'

The band turns out to be a woman trying to sing ballads with a man playing the piano and another on a slide guitar and it all doesn't work really well. An older man sitting near to us hears us groan. He leans over. 'The bands here aren't what they used to be,' he says. 'I remember the one they had here fifteen, twenty years ago. The lead guitarist would sing "Cracklin' Rosie" and it'd bring tears to your eyes. The girls here, they just used to melt.' Kate has stopped listening. I see she's being eyed by a guy leaning on the bar. She has noticed. He's got that glittery-eyed look she seems to go for.

His name's Roy and he knows a lot of anti-Aussie jokes. Kate and I exchange rolling eyes but I can see she's enjoying herself. I can't blame her. I've been worse than no company for days.

'Roy's going on to a party and he wants us to go with him,' Kate whispers.

'He wants you to go, you mean.'

'No – both of us. He said so.'

I don't want to go. She can tell. 'There's no law that says you can't have fun while you're looking for Emma.' Kate's impatient with me and her voice rises. One of Roy's mates lurches close to me.

'Who's Emma?' he shouts. 'You two got another beautiful Aussie chick hidden somewhere?'

I'm sure now. 'I'm going back to the motel,' I say firmly to Kate. 'Are you coming with me?'

'Oh, Ru-by,' she says. 'Can't you loosen up for once?'

Roy has his arm possessively around Kate's

shoulders. Some of his mates take up a chant of *Oh Rubee Oh Rubee*. I try to ignore it.

'Will you be okay, Kate?'

'Oh, sure.' She turns to Roy and waves her arm dismissively at me.

We've still got the rental car. I know the bill will be ticking up but I don't care. Rob will know what real expenses are once he has Evie for a wife.

I turn the car sharply into the motel entrance and nearly hit the name sign with the tin flap saying Vacancies which creaks when it's windy. Only two of the units are occupied, but I see another car parked by the reception door. A man leans by the door. Obviously he's pressed the outside bell and is waiting for an answer.

I walk unwillingly across the paving towards the waiting car. I can see a woman in the passenger seat and two kids in the back. They turn towards me. They all look exhausted.

The reception door opens and Mr Fraser appears. He looks tousled and annoyed at the disturbance but his face brightens when he sees me approaching. 'Ah, here's Ruby,' he says. 'She'll fix you up with a unit.' And disappears back into his flat, leaving the reception door standing open.

I fill out the form and hand the man the key to their unit and a container of milk. He looks at the milk doubtfully as I walk out with him and lock the reception door behind us. 'There's nowhere we can get a meal round here is there?'

I remember driving through the darkened small town only minutes before. 'I think even the pub's stopped serving food by now,' I say. 'But there's a kitchen in your unit. Have you got anything to cook?'

'No – we thought we'd get home to Auckland tonight,' the woman said from the car. 'But we're both too tired to drive any more.'

'You get settled in,' I tell them. 'I'll see what we've got to eat in our unit.'

I raid our kitchen and take them tomatoes and bacon and eggs, bread and butter. They look so worn out I almost offer to cook it for them.

So at last I'm alone in the unit. I flick on the TV and lie on the bed. The photo of Emma with her closed eyes is in my hands.

'I think you know lots you're not telling me, Miranda.'

*Isn't it strange how the other witness of Emma's drowning disappeared like that?*

'This isn't what I want to speak to you about.'

*Perhaps that witness never existed. After all we've only got Rob's word that he was there. We've only got Rob's word for all of it. It might have been Rob who got into difficulties and had to be rescued by Emma. Consider, Ruby, the guilt he'd be suffering. He'd be seeing you, day after day, year after year, knowing how you'd hate him if you found out it was his fault that Emma died.*

*Remember, Ruby, how he said that one day he was a carefree kid with a surfboard and within a week he was a family man with a mortgage? Perhaps it was all too much weight for him to carry. Perhaps after a year he'd had enough. Perhaps he deliberately waited a few minutes too long before trying to bring Emma's body back to life.*

It's impossible this picture Miranda's painting but the scene persists in front of my eyes.

'It's not true, Miranda. Rob loved Emma. He loved her so much it's still too painful for him to talk about her.'

*Painful, Ruby? Another way to avoid facing guilt. Refuse to talk about it.*

Miranda is wrong. Rob proved his huge love for Emma in the way he has always cared for me.

*Does he really care, Ruby? Five minutes after you go away from him he decides to marry someone you don't like.*

Once before, Miranda tried to get between Rob and me. She nearly succeeded those years ago in Hobart. She's not going to succeed this time. I hate the idea of Rob marrying Evie but I'm not allowing Miranda to poison all the years before.

I turn up the television and stare at it – an old Bette Davis tale of jealousy and spite and fierce revenge. Not the best thing to watch but there's not much choice. It's either that or rugby replays.

When I wake up again the TV is a hissing patch of blue snow in the corner. It must have been car doors outside the unit that woke me. I hear stifled laughing and 'Sssh! Sssh!' and then Kate's voice, 'Be quiet you'll get me fired' – there's an unmistakable sound of slurpy kissing right outside the door and I want to laugh.

A moment later a car door slams and the car slides away, the swing of its headlights crossing the curtains. Kate unlocks the door and tries to creep inside.

'I'm awake, Kate – it's okay. You can turn on the light.'

'Oh good, Ruby, I wanted to talk. I had a really great time. You should have come.'

She swishes around in the bathroom for a while and then hops into bed. She's asleep almost immediately. I'm left wide awake with Miranda's pictures moving in front of me over and over again.

I don't fall asleep properly until daybreak, and Kate has to wake me. She's smiling and brushing my nose with a twenty-dollar note.

'A present for you. Apparently you played Good Samaritan to some weary travellers last night and they left this for you. No wonder there was nothing here for breakfast this morning.'

'Sorry, Kate, I didn't think – '

'Don't worry! Now listen. I've got interesting news. Mr Fraser's going to take mummy Fraser and the ghastly Fraserettes up to Auckland to her mother's. And, because we're such *capable* girls, and especially after you were so helpful last night, he's going to leave us in charge here. On a proper wage at last. What do you think of that?'

She doesn't wait to find out. 'Not quite in charge. His father's going to shift into their place in case we have any problems, like nasty drunks or a bikie invasion, but basically we'll be on our own!'

'But, Kate, I was just thinking it was time we moved on – '

'Not yet, Ruby, please! Not right now, just when we're going to earn some real money – '

And not now you've just met Roy.

'Roy's really nice,' Kate says as if she'd heard me.

'If I'd known you were awake last night I'd have invited him in so you could get to know him properly. But then, he had to start work early this morning so it was just as well, I suppose.'

'What doing? Milking five hundred cows?'

'No no – he grows things. Cauliflowers or something. I don't know what he does to them first thing in the morning. Perhaps he washes them.'

Her eyes are dreamy with this idyllic rural scene. 'What's your letter, Kate?' There's an aerogram sticking out of her jeans pocket.

'Oh – I forgot! I think it's from Evie.'

I make two cups of coffee, my hands shaking, while Kate reads her letter. There's a long ominous silence from her. She's had time to read it four times over.

I put the coffee on the table and sit down opposite her. Here it comes.

'You've known for over a week that Evie's going to marry Rob and you didn't say a word! And it's such great news. Evie'll have a wonderful wedding. She says it'll be in Sydney because that's where all her friends are – Ruby?' She peers into my face and sees it all. 'Oh. You're not happy about this wedding. In fact you hate the whole idea like poison. *That's* why you were such a bitch to Rob on the phone.'

'Well, Evie rates pretty high on the bitch scale herself.' The words are out and I can't get them back.

Kate slams her cup down so hard that the coffee flies out and makes a huge brown slur on the lime-green wallpaper.

'That's my sister you're talking about.'

125

'I didn't mean to say that about Evie. I just mean she's much younger than he is – I mean she's our age!' – And she's been determined to get her claws into him ever since she set eyes on him last Christmas and I'll bet she never gave Rob my phone message. And I know why she paid Kate to get me out of the country – she wanted to put even more distance between Rob and me. While I'm thinking this, Kate's eyes narrow.

'You're jealous. That's what it is. You don't want Rob to be happy with anyone but you.'

'That's not true – '

'Oh, yes it is. You should just sit down and examine your feelings about Rob, Ruby. I think you want him for yourself.'

'That's *grotesque*!' I shout but she's already gone, and the slam of the door drowns the words.

## CHAPTER 14

S taying here is intolerable but I feel trapped, now that Kate's agreed to this crazy idea of looking after the motel for the Frasers.

Somehow – I don't know how – Kate and I maintain a truce for the rest of Saturday and between us get the motel work done. In the afternoon Roy comes to collect her, so it happens that I'm the one who gets the final instructions from Mr Fraser, and I meet Mr Fraser Senior minutes before the younger Frasers drive away in their clapped-out stationwagon.

I like old Mr Fraser. He's so different from his morose son. The motel's quiet that evening and we sit chatting in the Fraser's living room. We share a frozen chicken pic heated in the Fraser's oven which is only a little more efficient than the old models in the units. Perhaps it's because I don't want to be alone to – how did Kate put it? – examine my feelings about Rob. Perhaps it's because really I don't have anyone else to talk to. Mr Fraser's a completely detached stranger, a short round seventy-year-old in a faded blue denim

127

western shirt who will never come into my life again. Anyway, I find myself telling him everything. Well, not about Miranda. About the mystery of Emma. About being alone, anonymous, unattached.

Old Mr Fraser is a country and western music fanatic. He's brought a case of cassettes with him for his stay. As we talk into the evening he gets up often to slide in another tape as the previous one finishes.

Usually I hate this music. Tonight the wailing guitars and Emmylou Harris's sweet plaintiveness are part of the unreality.

Mr Fraser gets himself a bottle of beer from the kitchen and comes back wearing a real stetson cowboy hat and a string tie with a shiny medallion at his collar. It's too much. I can't stop laughing. He looks pleased and twirls an imaginary gun from an imaginary holster at his hip.

I laugh too much and it turns into tears. Mr Fraser gives me a red and white spotted handkerchief, folded with sharp ironed creases. 'It's my best cowboy hanky,' he says gravely. 'It's only since I've been retired I can wear my western gear. I won a trip to Disneyland back in the seventies and I brought it all back with me. Wore it first day back at work. Everyone cracked up just like you did. I had to go and change less than ten minutes into my shift.'

'What was your job?' Tears are gone. Now I'm stifling hiccups. 打嗝

'I've always been in the hospitality trade. The hotel industry. Hotel management, you know. Well, bar management mostly. An interesting job I always thought. I used to say you don't have to travel the world in this job – the world comes to you.'

'What sort of places did you work at?'

'Tourist centres mainly, I guess. Plenty of places down south, and over in Rotorua – down the road at Waitomo – '

'Waitomo Caves Hotel? You worked there?' With a jolt I'm back on the Emma trail.

'Sure I did. That's exactly the sort of place I liked to work. The world visits there.'

'You see, that's why I'm here. Emma, my mother, worked there years ago one summer. Probably 1967. Probably as a waitress in the restaurant.'

'Emma – what was her other name? Blake? Emma Blake.' He shakes his head. 'I don't recall the name. But it's a lot of years ago. Holiday workers came and went in droves. Lots of Aussie girls, hitching through New Zealand, just stayed long enough for expenses to get through to Auckland – '

'You mean you were there in 1967?' I'm probably too eager. He seems to back off a little.

'Sure was. Well, around then anyway. But, hang on, don't get your hopes up. I've said I don't recall the name – '

'Would you mind looking at a photo of her? Just in case you recognise her? It's a strange photo but if you recognise her it would be proof she had worked there – ' This pile of words trails behind me as I run back to the unit. There's a moment's panic when I don't find the photo in the drawer beside my bed. But I remember I'd fallen asleep the night before with it in my hands and sure enough, there it is, slipped to the floor behind the bed.

Old Mr Fraser holds the photo tilted towards the light. He tips his stetson to the back of his head.

'So she died, did she, the poor lass,' he says at last. 'Shame.'

I'm not sure what he means. 'Do you recognise her?' He must be able to hear my heart thumping.

'It's the name that bothers me, you see. I remember the face, all right. But I don't recall the name Emma Blake. I don't think she was an Aussie, either.'

'Can you remember where she came from?'

He puts down the photo and shakes his head. 'It was a long time ago. It might come to me. I'm not as young as I was. Give it time, give it time.' He goes through to the fridge and brings back another bottle. I eye it sourly. That stuff probably killed the very brain cell that contained my mother's name. I wonder if he's simply humouring me, unwilling to disappoint with a simple no, I don't remember her.

'She wasn't travelling, that was what was different. Not one of these backpackers as they call them now. She was earning money, saving for something. I know. I've got it. She was saving up for her wedding.' He looked across the table at me, closely, as if he hasn't seen me properly before. 'There's even a bit of a resemblance, now that it's pointed out to me.'

He could be having me on. He's got the photo to compare me with. But even if – and I hardly dare to linger on this possibility – even if he's really remembering Emma, I know there's no point in rushing him.

I wait while he puts on another tape. *Don't wanna ride no shootin' star* the words go before Mr Fraser speaks again.

'She came from the east coast, over Waihi way. She was dead keen on marrying a young Maori chap she was crazy about.'

'How can you remember all this, Mr Fraser? Over the years you must have met hundreds of girls working for a few weeks in various pubs. I don't believe you'd remember them all like this. Just from a photo. Especially a photo like that.' I'm struggling to speak calmly, to keep the hope off my face.

'Well, she was memorable, that one.' He looks again at the photo of Emma's dead face. 'It's a bit sad to see her looking like this. She was a livewire. And kind. She was kind to people, you know? You don't meet that many people in this world who are kind, plain and ordinary kind. Specially not among the younger ones.'

Again I wonder if he's romancing to make me feel good. 'Can you remember anyone else who was working there at the same time? Someone who might remember her name?'

He doesn't seem to hear. He's looking at the photo again. 'How did she die? Did you tell me?'

'She drowned.'

'Terrible thing.' He's looking troubled.

'Mr Fraser? Can you remember anyone else who worked there when you did?'

He rouses himself. 'Let me see. There was old Sparky White, the manager. He's dead now. Retired and went to Tauranga a few years back. Dropped dead from doing nothing. There was a young chap running the restaurant – he'd remember her for sure. Can't think of his name. Anyway I heard he went off to Queensland years ago.' He sighs and shakes his head. 'The old memory starts to go, you know? If I could just remember her name . . .'

'Could Blake be her married name?'

'Not if she married her Waihi bloke, it wouldn't.' He looks at my face speculatively, and I realise he's looking for traces of Maori ancestry. 'That's another reason to remember her, I guess. Back in those days it was noticed more, you know? A pakeha girl marrying a Maori, you remarked on that, specially round here in the country. Looking at you though I wonder if she did marry him in the end. Can't see any Maori in you. And anyway,' he hands the photo back to me, 'it's the Emma that's wrong, too. I can't recall her as Emma.'

'Was it – was the name Miranda by any chance?' My voice is deliberately casual to hide my feelings.

'Miranda? No. Something like that though.' He leans back, closes his eyes and tips his stetson forward, making experimental 'mmm' sounds with his lips shut. 'Magda,' he says suddenly.

'Magda?'

'That's it.' He pushes his hat back as his eyes snap open triumphantly. 'Magda . . . Brady.'

Magda Brady. I whisper the name, turning my head so he can't see the rush of tears. I thought before that he was inventing, embroidering a faint memory to comfort me, but now he must be truly remembering.

Nobody could be so cruel as to invent a name in these circumstances. And the name feels right. It settles in my mind as if it belonged there. I have the same feeling of truth as I did when Miranda told me the cloak was Emma's. Magda's.

It's nearly eleven o'clock when I say goodnight to old Mr Fraser. I pause beside the phone in reception, calculating the time. It's only about nine o'clock in Australia.

But I don't want to ring Rob. I have to tell someone about Magda. But not Kate, either. I think of Gran. I'll phone her. I have to share this excitement with someone.

'Ruby! How lovely to hear your voice, dear. I've been checking the post every day for a letter – '

'Gran – this is a really bad line. There's an echo – can you hear me?' I can hear my own voice echoing back a second later. 'I had to phone – I'm so excited – '

'Are you, dear? I'm so relieved you feel that way about it – '

'Gran – ' I try to interject, puzzled, but she's talking on.

' – because I'm so, so pleased for Rob. He'll be happy and settled at last. I haven't met Evie yet but I've seen photos of her and she looks such a pretty girl, such a *successful* girl. Now. When will you be coming home? They haven't set the exact date but it won't be far away. Rob and Evie will want you to be a bridesmaid and of course we'll have to see about your dress – '

'Gran!' She doesn't hear me.

' – be best if you fly into Sydney since that's where the wedding's to be. Rob's going to take a suite at a hotel there for us but then he's probably told you all that already. You just get yourself organised on a flight, dear.'

'Gran?'

'Oh dear, I can hardly hear you at all. Now Rob tells me you feel you've reached a dead end on your search, dear. I'm so sorry about that. But I'm glad you're pleased about the wedding. You deserve a bit of fun.'

I've been trying to break in but my voice isn't getting through. There doesn't seem to be any point in persisting. I can't bear any more. I say goodbye and stare at the dead receiver in my hand for moments. Everyone I know is going mad. I'm the only one still in a circle of sanity.

By five in the morning I've decided what to do. Kate hasn't returned but I know she will. I pack all my things. As the sky lightens with daybreak I put my bags in the back seat of the car.

*Dear Mr Fraser,*

*Thank you for your company last evening. Now that I know her real name I'm satisfied and I'm free now to return to Australia. I phoned my grandmother last night and she wants me to get back as soon as possible so forgive my hasty exit! Kate is very capable and I'm sure she'll be able to manage the motel work on her own.*

*Thanks again for last night. Can I ask you to keep my questions about my mother a secret between us?*

*Regards,*

*Ruby Summerton*

I leave the note for Mr Fraser on the reception desk, pinned under the phone.

I try to write a note for Kate but can't think what to say. So I leave her nothing.

It's a short drive to the city of Hamilton through the murky dawn. No sunrise, just a lightening of the low grey clouds.

I'd been counting on leaving the rental car at the office in the city and renting another from some other company. But it's Sunday and everything seems to be closed. I could leave the car – post the keys through the door – but no offices are open for me to get another car. At least I couldn't find one.

I drive across a bridge and along a road following the river. I'm aware of large houses with gracious gardens and flowering trees, other trees with autumn-coloured leaves, but really my mind is ticking over possibilities.

It's probably not a good idea to rent another car, anyway. I'd still have to use Rob's credit card to get it.

I stop the car near a grassy picnic area by the river. I get into the back seat and sort through my clothes.

Then I start on my shoulder bag. The large wad of New Zealand dollars I'd drawn on Rob's card is hardly touched. I still have three Australian hundred-dollar notes hidden in a secret pocket deep in my bag. That leaves the credit card itself, and my driver's licence, my passport, my diary.

I keep the diary, just rip out that front page I filled in so carefully with all the details of my old identity.

The other things are difficult to destroy. Those plastic credit cards and drivers' licences and the reinforced card of the passport are built to last. Then I remember my nail scissors. Even with them it takes a long time to end up with a pile of unrecognisable fragments. But by then nobody could solve this jigsaw puzzle. Ruby Summerton's gone.

I scatter the pieces in the metal drum for rubbish on the edge of the picnic-site.

On the way to the rental-car depot I see the other thing I need: a St Vincent de Paul bin for cast-off clothes. I take my bigger bag from the back of the car and stuff it into the opening at the top of the bin, pushing and squeezing at its corners till it disappears inside. Goodbye dresses and spare shirts, denim overalls with the million pockets. I never liked you anyway.

Getting rid of the car is far easier. I lock it up and drop the keys through the hole in the depot door.

So I stand on the footpath with a small shoulder bag and another bag, not much bigger, gloriously light. I'm wearing the cloak. I have a fair bit of anonymous cash in my shoulder bag. There's nothing with me that can say who I am, where I came from.

*Don't wanna ride no shootin' star, just wanna play on m'rhythm guitar.* I sing the words to myself. I'm like Emma all those years ago in Australia. The only difference is I don't have a baby in my arms.

Not Emma. Magda.

*I'll* be Emma Blake now.

Magda. It's beautiful. I don't know anything about the name. Perhaps it's from Mary Magdalen. I've never known anyone called Magda so I have no preconceptions about it. Magda. My mother's name. I treasure the sound.

## CHAPTER 15

Time's short; I don't know how long I'll be allowed to remain lost.

But then, perhaps it'll be days before they notice, weeks, maybe. Kate will get the information I've gone back to Australia. Gran will think I'm booking a flight and I'm on my way. As for Rob, well, he seems to have other things to think about. I expect it will be months before he wonders where I am.

Anyway, where would they look? I'm not Ruby Summerton now. By the time they start wondering – if they ever do – old Mr Fraser will have left the Avalon Motel and no one would think of contacting him for information. And Kate will be too busy with the motel to run on her own and with her new boyfriend to get to know Mr Fraser well. I'm glad I didn't let Kate get the police involved with my search.

I head for a bus terminal two blocks from the car depot. It makes sense to me to go first to the town Mr Fraser told me about. Knowing her name seems a magic key.

The bus terminal is quiet. No queues or revving buses. There's a woman reading behind the ticket counter.

'What time's the next bus to Waihi?'

'You'll be waiting a while. Ten o'clock tomorrow. Monday.'

I should have expected that but all the same my face must show something because she goes on, 'I could get you to Auckland later or down south later still, but that's it for today.'

'But it doesn't look far on the map . . . is there a train?'

She laughs. 'You find a train to Waihi and you'll be finding something no one else has for a lot of years.'

I turn away from the ticket counter. For a couple of seconds I regret the car keys lying on the floor inside the locked door of the rental-car depot. But Magda had managed alone, and so shall I.

'Over from Australia, are you, dear?' the woman calls. I turn back, astonished. Is it that obvious? Is it my accent?

'No,' I say with a faked little laugh, speaking carefully. 'I'm from – from the South Island. On holiday.'

'I could give you some addresses of places to stay that aren't too expensive, if that's the problem.' She's looking at me doubtfully. Perhaps I look unusual.

'No, no.' I laugh again. Probably this is what Magda learned to do. Invent laughs and small lies for strangers. 'There's no problem. I've got friends here I can stay with. Bye!'

I leave the place quickly looking as if I've no cares. Already there's been too much talk. I've the feeling she won't forget me, and if they come looking for me, tracing me from the place I'd left the car, the bus station would be obvious –

But then I remember they won't come looking for me.

All the same, I'm feeling conspicuous in the cloak. Away from the curious eyes of the woman at the bus depot, I take it off and push it into my bag. I replace it with an anonymous red wind shirt. It's not as warm, but it will do.

There's a row of cabs in the main street. 'Can you take me to the edge of town on the road to Waihi?'

'Right. Hop in.'

I sit in the back, my bag on the seat beside me. The driver's glancing at me in his rear-vision mirror.

'Not thinking of hitching, are you?' he asks suddenly.

'Oh, no. Some friends are giving me a ride.'

'Glad to hear it. Wouldn't like to see any daughter of mine hitching a lift.'

I'm annoyed with myself. I seem to be leaving clues everywhere. I wish I'd looked at the map first and used the name of some other town on the same road.

He stops past a roundabout. I pay him and stand back from the road on the footpath, making a show of looking at my watch but out of the corner of my eye making sure he's driving away. He seems to linger within watching distance unnecessarily long. What if he parks somewhere he can see me? Well, so what? He can't stop me hitchhiking. It's not against the law.

But finally he's gone. I walk along the footpath for a short distance, feeling self-conscious. I've never done this before. I'm forced into it when the footpath ends. There's the sound of a car from behind. I hold out my thumb, my arm stiff and not very far from my side, not daring to look around.

The car doesn't stop. A row of kids' faces jeer at me through the back window.

I walk a long way. The cars speed past and no one stops. At least it's not raining.

But I'm so hungry. It's midday and I've had nothing, not even a cup of coffee, since the chicken pie with Mr Fraser last night. The road stretches ahead with no sign of a shop or a filling station. A hot meat pie and a can of something sweet and fizzy. Fish and chips and a donut. I'm in a paradise of junk food when I notice a car has pulled off the road just ahead of me. It's a low red car which looks new and powerful, driven by a middle-aged man. He reaches across to open the passenger door. I lean in to get a look at him.

'Going far?' he asks.

He looks okay, staid and business-like. 'Waihi,' I reply.

'You're in luck. I'm driving right past there.'

If he turns unpleasant I'll make him stop at a filling station, I decide. Say I'm desperate to go to the toilet.

He drives extremely fast. 'Cops have a day off on Sunday,' he says. 'I hope.'

Apart from that he doesn't say anything, and that suits me. I remember reading somewhere that if people pick up hitchhikers it's because they want company and making interesting conversation is required as a kind of payment for the lift. But I don't want to talk and if he must have conversation he'll have to start it. Also I'm concentrating on how the road is flashing past far too fast. He seems to be overtaking everything and often recklessly.

He swings the car to the left, a side road that stretches in a straight line as far as I can see.

'Where are you going? Why have you turned off the main road?'

'This is a short cut. The swamp road. You must be a stranger around here. Everyone knows this road. You can really put your foot down on this road.'

He sounds relaxed, and I push away my alarm and try to relax too. He's driving even faster, but the road seems empty and dead straight.

But there is a corner, and he takes it too fast. A small herd of dairy cows is mooching along, covering the road. The driver curses and slams on the brakes. The cows bellow and rear, their eyes rolling white. He misses them but the car leaps over the soft grassy verge and ploughs into a fence. For a few seconds we sit stunned, catching the breath that was pushed out by the bite of the seat belts.

Then the driver jumps out, and stooping, runs around to my door. 'Hurry,' he orders, wrenching open the door, 'get in the driver's seat.'

'*What?*'

'As if you were driving! Come on!' He's crouched by the open passenger door.

142

I get out of the car, my bag and shoulder bag in my arms. 'I will not.'

'Look,' he says, 'do me a favour – I'll have to get a tow truck and that means I'll have to report the accident!'

'So? No one's hurt. What's the problem?'

The problem is that he's disqualified. Not supposed to be driving. Had his licence taken off him for a year.

'For speeding, I suppose,' I say.

'Something like that,' he mutters.

I tell him I'm not going to pretend I was driving. Then I remember my destroyed driver's licence. 'Anyway, I haven't got a licence myself. I don't know how to drive.'

'I don't *believe* it,' he says, his eyes going up to heaven.

I say that if he hadn't given me a lift he would have been on his own and wouldn't have had someone to blame for the accident. He says he'll probably have to go to jail. I say he drives like a maniac and deserves to. So we're arguing by the wrecked car when the young farmer who's supposed to be looking after the cows roars up on his motorbike. By now the cows are calm and munching the lush roadside grass.

'Got a problem?' The farmer's quick intelligence grasps the situation at a glance, I say to myself. I mean, isn't it obvious there's a problem? A car buried in the ditch, two people shouting at each other –

The man gets his words in first. 'Women drivers,' he says in a disgusted voice. He and the farmer exchange knowing glances.

I manage a laugh. 'I told you, I can't drive. Thanks for the lift, I don't think. I hope I see you coming next time.' I walk away. Of course this is all bravado. I've been running on adrenalin for ten minutes now. I'm shaking inside.

The driver could stick to his story and he and the farmer could easily overtake me. It's got the potential for a great mess. I can't prove I wasn't driving. I can't even prove who I am.

But they don't follow me. I quickly look back and the two are deep in conversation. With any luck they've forgotten about me. What I need now is another lift. The road remains empty.

I need something to eat, too. I'm dizzy and my bag suddenly seems too heavy. The road's endless. I put my things down and get out my map. It's no help. There's a network of country roads and I could be on any one of them. And somehow the day seems to be ending. The heavy clouds which haven't shifted all day won't give me any clue where the sun is. My watch has gone. Maybe it flew off in the car accident when I flung my arms out at the moment of impact. It could be nearly sunset. It might be dark soon. No sleep last night, no food all day, no watch.

But here's a car. It slides gently to a stop and a woman with short grey hair winds down the passenger window and calls back to me. 'Would you like a lift, dear?'

The back seat of the car has soft cushions and a mohair rug. It's warm, and there's a sweet scent of apples. I'm struggling to keep my eyes open and answer their questions. I know I should be more cagey but I've lost all my defences in weariness. It's even overcome the growls of hunger. I have to respond to these two women's warmth and concern. So I end up admitting I don't know where I'm going to stay in Waihi.

They take over. I don't remember much more about that evening. There's hot delicious soup that I'm too tired to do more than sip at, and then the warm bed in their spare room. They watch over me as I finally drift off to sleep. The last thing I remember is the gentle voice of one of them. 'What's your name, dear?'

'Emma,' I murmur, then I'm asleep.

## CHAPTER 16

Of course when I wake up it takes minutes to put it all together, to recall where I am. It doesn't help when I hear 'Good morning, Emma!' and in walks one of the two women with a cup of tea.

I can only stare – didn't they tell me their names? – and then say thank you as she draws back the curtains. The morning sun is blinding.

'You can help yourself to breakfast when you come down, dear. Just when you're ready.' She's gone. I crawl out of bed and look through the window, flinching at the brightness. There's a garden set out below, an intricacy of cobbled paths, arches garlanded with climbing roses, an encircling shelter of thick shrubs with dark leaves glinting in the sun. As the morning light dries the dew, sweet smells drift up to the open window. At last, I know what to do next. The quest seems less a matter of obsession, more one of reason. I'm getting very close, Miranda, with or without your help. Not long now.

The women's names are Dulcie and Violet. They're

retired schoolteachers from Wellington, shifted here just eighteen months ago. As I thank them for looking after me last night, I'm thinking over how much to tell them. They're newcomers to this area, wouldn't know people – in particular a person named Magda Brady – who'd lived here nearly twenty years ago. But they've been kind, and I feel safe and comfortable here. What's more, they don't ask any questions. They aren't full of advice and warnings. This lack of prying makes me feel guilty. I can't stand up and walk away. I have to make some explanation.

'I've come to Waihi to find out about someone who lived here a while ago. She might have gone to school here, perhaps married here. It's important, that's why I couldn't wait for the bus – why I started hitching yesterday. I am in Waihi, aren't I?'

'Five minutes from the Waihi Post Office, Emma,' Violet or Dulcie answers. Already I've forgotten which was which. I who should know how important names are.

'We'll be going to the shops in a little while,' the other one says. 'We could show you where the courthouse is, if you like.'

'The courthouse?'

'Oh, well, we don't mean to interfere. But it's the best place to start, don't you think? The registry of births and marriages?'

'And, Emma dear, that's a pretty blouse – doesn't it look charming, Violet, that lacy collar with those severe smart blue jeans?' I look at her closely but she's not being sarcastic, she really means it. 'But the wind outside is very sharp. If you've got something warm, perhaps you should fetch it just in case.'

Dulcie was right. An hour later I'm huddled in my cloak on the corner of Kenny Street, shivering in the cold wind that cuts through the sunlight. But it would have seemed right to wear the cloak anyway. And my jade earrings. And by now, in just an hour, I've learned so much.

The names were there, the registration of the marriage. Sonny David Manuatu was married to Magda Blake Brady on 14 March 1967. There were two addresses. There was the registration of Madga's birth in 1949 with the same address as the one shown with her marriage.

I asked the official at the courthouse if he knew the address. Was it far away? It was important that I found it.

'There's no one there,' he told me. 'It's been empty for years.' Then his face brightened. He's got a nice face, I notice, even while there's so much for me to attend to, and glossy brown hair cut short. 'Oh – are you an interested party in the property?'

'What do you mean?'

'Well, it's no secret. It's been advertised in the local paper by the council. The house is about to be repossessed by the council in default of rates payment.'

'What?' He must have thought I was slow but he shouldn't talk jargon.

'Nobody's paid the rates for years. So they advertise and if no one claims the property and pays up the rates, the local council can sell it. It's quite a normal practice.'

'How soon will all this happen?'

'You'd have to see the council about that. It's not really our department. I only know about it because my grandfather's thinking of bidding if it goes to auction. He's into local history. Writes articles for the local paper sometimes. He says that old house has got a history. He calls it the Emma Blake house. It should be preserved, he says – hey, are you all right?'

'*Emma Blake?*'

'Yeah. Apparently this Emma Blake was some nineteenth-century character who caused some stirs around here – are you sure you're okay?'

I might have been dizzy with excitement but I managed to ask him again how to get to the house. He started to tell me how to drive there, and I said I didn't have a car. He drew me a careful map. Too far to walk, he told me.

I asked him about the other address, the one with Sonny Manuatu's name, the man Magda married. It was at Waihi Beach, he explained. Another town, really. On the coast, fifteen minutes' drive away –

So I'm standing on the corner near the post office, counting the dollars in my bag. I'm going to find a taxi. I'm too close to finding out who Magda was to wait around for a bus, to risk hitching. Things are happening fast now. I was right to become Emma.

There's a phone box outside the post office. I look up the taxi number, but on the way through the alphabet I pause at the Ms. There it is. Manuatu, S D. The same address I have written down. Sonny David. I don't have the nerve to telephone. I don't know what I'd say.

149

For ten minutes we drive through hilly farming country, sheep grazing, past an apple orchard. Magda must have often travelled on this road, looked at the same stand of pines on the crest of a hill that I now see. The road turns sharply and there's the sea, glittering, bright blue, a black island centred on the sharp horizon. Down the twisting road on the other side of the hill we go, and then the driver is following streets of small houses on small blocks of land and suddenly the sea seems a long way from here again. But I can hear it and smell it. There is salt spray in the air and the sound of breakers when he slows and stops the taxi.

'Do you want me to wait?' he asks.

The house looks quiet. Red geraniums in pots are lined along the porch at the front. There's a tidy concrete path to a front door but not a car parked anywhere. Perhaps, probably, no one's home. But as I watch from the taxi I see a curtain twitch at the window beside the front door.

I pay the taxi-driver and tell him not to wait. The cold wind is fierce. I fling the flying corner of my cloak over the other shoulder and walk steadily to the front door. There's a door knocker in the shape of a fox's head. It makes a dull metallic clack.

The door opens. It's shadowy inside. Someone stands there. 'You,' she says. She turns and I can see her moving away from me down the hallway to the back of the house.

She leaves the door open, so I follow. The sun-light's shining strongly into the kitchen where I find her. She's sitting in a straightbacked chair beside the table. Small, white-haired, severe, a Maori woman wearing spectacles which throw two circles of reflected light.

I stand there and we're both still for I don't know how long.

'No. You're not Magda, now I get a look at you. But you're wearing her things.'

'I'm Ruby. Magda's daughter.'

She breaks into laughter. It's terrifying.

'You're not Ruby,' she says. 'Ruby was the daughter that Magda really loved, not you. You're not Ruby. You're Miranda. That's your name.'

'Miranda?' I whisper. The room grows cold. I shrink inside the cloak. I catch sight of myself reflected in the glass doors of a cupboard. A pinched white face shivering in a black wrap. I'm Miranda?

'Ruby's dead,' the voice from the chair goes on. 'Ruby died when she was one year old. On her first birthday. Ruby died while your trashy mother was out making you in the back seat of some pakeha's car.' Her voice rises to a shriek.

Some minutes later she speaks again, her voice quieter, but mocking. 'Do you want me to show you Ruby's grave?'

No – no – no: I don't know if I say this. The front door's still open, waiting to get rid of me from this house as soon as possible. I'm out on the road and somehow find a track to the beach.

There's the noise of the waves and the windborne sand stings and sticks to the tears on my face. I don't know how long I sit there in the black tent of my cloak. Ruby's dead. *I'm* Miranda.

There's someone sitting beside me. Perhaps he's been there for a while. I see brown feet in black kung fu shoes frayed at the toes. Muscled legs. Faded black footie shorts. A face watching me with brown eyes, black hair streaked grey tied back in a ponytail. 'Mum said I'd find you here,' he says. 'I'm sorry if she was rough on you. But you can't blame us for getting a shock. It's years since Magda left. And you turn up, wearing her stuff. You're so like her. You could be Magda.'

Magda – Ruby – Emma – Miranda. I'm losing grip on who I am.

## CHAPTER 17

'I'm Sonny Manuatu. You'd be Magda's second daughter. Miranda.'

It's as if I'd spoken my last thoughts aloud.

'She always called me Ruby,' I say after a while. 'I've always thought I was Ruby. And now that woman says it was me who was Miranda all along.' There's an enormity about being Miranda that I can't think about properly yet.

'You mustn't worry about what Mum says.' Sonny stands up and reaches out his hand. He helps me up. He brushes away the sand stuck to my face. His eyes stay for a moment on the jade earrings but he says nothing about them. 'That cloak. She blew a whole summer's wages as a waitress on that cloak. And now you have it. What shall I call you, then?'

'I don't know.'

'I'll take you to see Magda's house. Would you like that?'

There are a million things for Sonny Manuatu and I to say to each other on the drive back to Waihi from

153

the beach but we're silent. I'm too overwhelmed to say anything. Perhaps he is too. Maybe not. It could all be too far in the past for him to care about now. Probably he's got a new family.

He stops the van beside the road but I can't see any house. 'It's over there, beyond that hill. Not far, just a couple of minutes' walk. The hill hides it from the road. That's probably what's saved it from break-ins all these years. Nobody knows it's there.'

The hill protects the house from the wind as well as thieves. It's an old single-storeyed house nestled into its encircling hill as if it had grown there. Its wood is so weathered it's impossible to tell what colour it was. The garden's a chaos of weeds. But the house doesn't look abandoned. All of the windows are blank with closed curtains. To me it looks as if it's sleeping.

The sun's warm away from the wind. I sit on a stone bench under an apple tree, unpruned for years, just a handful of misshapen fruit to show for this year's crop.

'They told me the house might be auctioned,' I say.

Sonny sits beside me. 'I know. I feel bad about that. I looked after it for a few years after she left, paid the rates, kept it ready for her. But then I lost heart. Do you think she'll want to come back here? I'd make sure it was kept for her if she was coming back.' He doesn't know she's dead. He goes on before I can think how to answer him. 'Did she send you back to see if the house was okay?'

'Sonny, are you my father?'

'Is that what Magda told you?'

'Magda didn't tell me anything! Sonny, a few hours

ago I didn't even know your name, or that this place existed. I only found out Magda's real name two days ago.'

'Miranda, you've only got to look into a mirror to see I'm not your dad. Well, it's pretty unlikely.'

'I thought that too,' I mumble.

'We could go on and on asking each other questions – you tell me what you do know.'

'Well, I should tell you first, Sonny, that – that Magda died. Seventeen years ago now.'

He doesn't say anything, just rests his elbows forward on his knees and studies his hands.

I tell him how Rob discovered Magda and me the day I was one year old, that they set up house and had a year together, but that when she died Rob knew no more about her past life than he did the day he met her; his adopting me legally when all the efforts to trace her relations got nowhere. And that nobody at all had considered a New Zealand connection until a chance remark about the jade earrings.

'My present to her when we got married.' It's the first thing he's said while I've been telling him all I know.

'It's your turn to tell me your story,' I say. 'There's a lot I don't understand. I don't understand the things your mother said.'

He looks at his hands again, and my mind flits back over the weeks and months before this moment when I never thought I'd get this far.

'I'm trying to think what to say to you. I'm thinking, here's Miranda, come back here after all these years, and she'll want to know the truth. You should have the truth, Miranda; it's your right. But, that's a big job you're giving me.'

'What do you mean?' Is he going to tell me nothing? And the name Miranda still shakes me.

'You know how your memory can play tricks. Your present brain can change the past. When we tell our own past stories, we can never be sure how much we're deceiving ourselves.' My bewilderment must be all over my face. He suddenly smiles. 'Don't look so concerned. They all say I spend so much time thinking I never get to the point. That's why I like fishing. Fish don't complain if you sit all day, forget to put the hook in the water. And Magda never minded. She and I used to discuss and argue hour after hour. She said I should be up at the university doing my thinking and arguing. But school was never good for me.'

'Where did you meet Magda?'

He smiles again. 'Good move, girl. Get me back to the point. We were at high school together. We liked each other right from the beginning. I never doubted we'd get married, have kids, live by the beach for ever. Magda liked the water. She was a really good swimmer. That's how I remember her most – coming out of the pool or the sea, long hair slicked back, eyes wide open with her eyelashes all spikey, beads of water on her shiny skin. She was winning races all over the place. Over in Hamilton, up in Auckland. She even won some scholarship. A year's training in Auckland. We used to joke how she'd be swimming in the Mexican Olympics.'

'Did she take the scholarship?' I'm shivering, but it's not cold in the sun. I think it's excitement. Already Sonny's words have put more flesh and blood on my mother than I've ever known before.

'Well, no. We – ah, you know how it is, we got carried away a few times and then the next thing is Magda's expecting. So. She never made it to Auckland.'

*She never made it to Auckland.* An Olympic ambition dismissed in that simple sentence. 'What did Magda think about that?'

'She had the baby to think about, didn't she.' He shrugged. 'We were starting our family. That was what was important to her. She was living here with her grandparents. They weren't pleased with our news.' He chuckled. 'There was all hell for a while there. Magda moved over to our place, started living with Mum and me at the beach.'

Her grandparents? I wonder why not her parents, but I leave that till later, not wanting to distract Sonny from his story of Magda.

'Round about here I made a big mistake. I went off and joined the army. It meant I was away a lot and Magda didn't like that. At the time it seemed the only choice, the only way I could get a good job, provide for Magda. Be a good husband. Then there was the baby too, the one we called Ruby.' I can't suppress a sudden gasp. When you've had a name all your life, it's hard to realise it's not really yours; it belonged to someone else all the time.

'You should have seen Magda with that baby. It was as if it was all she'd ever wanted. We thought it would be a good time to get married. Magda said she wanted to get some savings together first, and off she went to work as a live-in waitress at a pub at Waitomo over the summer. Ruby stayed with Mum.'

It doesn't add up to me, doesn't make sense the way Sonny's telling it. If Magda was so happy with Ruby, how could she leave her for so long? But once again I don't interrupt.

'Anyway Magda came back after the summer – with that big black cloak.' He laughs. 'So much for savings. We got married. Then suddenly things got bad. New Zealand had got itself involved in the Vietnam War. My artillery unit was being sent over. I had to go.' He sighs and pauses for a few seconds. 'I didn't know till then what hard feelings Magda had for war, fighting, for my job. We argued but it wasn't like the arguments we used to have. These were fierce and furious. Real ding-dongs. She tried to persuade me to disappear, to go bush for a year or two until it all blew over. She wouldn't understand when I said I couldn't do that. Sometimes it was as if the hate she had for war spilled over on to me. It was me she was hating.'

I can tell the story's getting harder for him to tell. He often halts, clenching and stretching his fingers.

'I had to go finally two days before my baby's first birthday. The rest is what I put together from what Mum told me. The first day I was gone Magda stayed in her bed, refused to eat or talk or tend to Ruby. The next day, Ruby's birthday, she put on her lipstick and her big black cloak and went to town. She didn't come back until the next day. Mum said she could tell the minute Magda walked in that next morning. Mum reckons she knows these things. She wasn't surprised nine months later when Magda gave birth and she knew it wasn't my baby.'

'But what about Ruby? Your mother said –'

'Ruby died during that night Magda was away. No particular reason. Ruby wasn't sick or anything. These days, they call them cot deaths. It nearly broke Mum's heart. She loved Ruby.'

'I expect Magda didn't feel very happy about it either.'

'Well, you see, Miranda, I don't know, I wasn't there, and I never saw Magda again. I get back from Nam and find my wife's gone, and my baby daughter's in a grave.'

'Your mother drove Magda away.'

'No. She wouldn't have done that. You've got Mum all wrong.'

'Oh, really? She called my mother trashy.'

'Listen to me! She saw Magda as her daughter! Magda was *family* as far as Mum was concerned. And so were you. Magda ran away and took you. She didn't ever let Mum know where she was, if she was safe, if you were safe. That's what makes Mum bitter. That's why she said what she did to you. And don't forget she's getting on a bit. Seeing you like that gave her a shock, opened up all that old hurt. Seeing you would have shaken me up a bit too, I can tell you, if she hadn't warned me. As it was . . .' His voice drops away.

'The thing is,' he goes on after a moment, 'if Magda hadn't run away, you'd have grown up as our daughter, Mum's beloved mokopuna. When I got home and found Magda gone, I wished I'd been left there rotting in that shitty jungle like half my mates.'

Dimly I can see that he's hurting, that I've appeared from nowhere and brought him back to pain he dealt with years ago. But my own mind is reeling from so much, and right now I have to be by myself. I can't take in any more.

'Give me the key to the house, Sonny. I'd like to have a look inside.' I leave him sitting on the bench in the garden. I hadn't meant this quest of mine to hurt anyone else.

It's cool inside the house. A draught follows me in through the doorway and the curtains shiver. There is an answering whisper from the shadows around the black coal range.

I push aside the long curtains which conceal a bay window, disturbing ancient cobwebs. Dust billows from the fabric and dances in the sudden rush of sunshine. I can see my footprints across the dust-covered floor. I'm the first one here for years.

There's a hallway with closed doors, two on each side. At the end is an outside door with panels of coloured glass. In each room I draw back the curtains, filling the rooms with light. The first is a sitting room. The huge carved fireplace has been boarded up and there's a two-bar electric heater fitted on the hearth. In the corner there's an enormous old-fashioned television, its top crowded with ornaments and some photographs in silver frames.

In the bedrooms piles of blankets lie folded on the ends of the beds. There are clothes hanging in the wardrobes. There's another room which looks part office, part storeroom. A heap of suitcases sits in one corner, there's a desk by the window, a steel filing cabinet in another corner; papers and books are jammed into a bookcase which covers one wall. Through this room's window I see the bench in the garden where I'd been sitting with Sonny. He's not there now.

I don't know how long I've been in the house, standing in each room, not looking at anything in particular but just feeling it. I have not picked up the photographs and brushed away the dust to see them properly, not yet. From the look of the outside of the house I'd been expecting a colonial farmhouse with its furniture and decorations unchanged from the nineteenth century. But of course generations have lived here, each generation altering the house in tune with its taste and fashion; generations of my own family.

Sonny is in the kitchen, tracing a pattern in the dust on the table. As if I'd done it a hundred times before, I fetch a cloth from the big cupboard by the coal range and wipe the dust from the table's surface. The wood starts to gleam. I want to keep going, to polish each of its turned legs and then start on the floor. Later, I tell myself.

'Do you own this house, Sonny?'

'I suppose so. I've never really thought. Well, I've

thought of it as Magda's, since her grandparents left it to her. There's no one else. Except you. Perhaps it's yours.'

It's the idea that's been growing ever since I saw the place. I want to live here.

## CHAPTER 18

$D$ ulcie and Violet are gathering flowers in the late afternoon-shadowed garden when Sonny drops me back at their house, calling 'See you tomorrow, Miranda' as he drives off in a roar of faulty exhaust pipe.

'But we thought your name was Emma, dear,' Dulcie says as we go inside. I catch a glance between the women as if Violet's reproving Dulcie for her curiosity.

'That was just for a little while. The day before yesterday I was Ruby. But now I find out I've been Miranda all along.'

'Well, Miranda. Anyway, dear, there's no need to ask if you've had a successful day. It's written all over your face.'

'I haven't found out everything. Far from it. But I know lots more about Magda, and I've found her house. And I'm going to live there for a while. But the power won't be connected until tomorrow, so I was wondering if I could stay with you for another night?'

They say of course that's all right. 'Is it an empty house you're moving into, Miranda?'

'Oh, no, I think it's got everything that I need. I'll have to get some groceries, that's all.'

'What Dulcie meant was will you be living there on your own?'

'Of course.' I see them swap looks again. They can talk without words.

'Are you sure that's a good idea?'

'I won't be lonely. I'm used to being on my own.' Right now I can't wait to be on my own, to think about what I've found out from Sonny. I go upstairs to bed soon after dinner, but the long day overtakes me and I'm asleep as soon as I put out the light.

Sonny arrives the next morning. He has a surprise for me. It's a brownish-grey puppy with huge furry feet and ears, heartbreaking brown eyes.

'Oh, Sonny. What's his name?'

'Hasn't got one yet. If you like him, he's yours. You can name him.'

'But I've never had a dog before. How will I know how to look after him?'

'I'll give you a hand to train him. Don't worry, in a couple of months he'll be looking after you.'

I can tell Dulcie and Violet approve of the dog. I realise they've been worrying if I'll be safe on my own. They've given me a basket of roses and daisies, a pot plant and a flowering creeper to plant near a verandah post. I tell them to visit me soon, and turn back to wave as Sonny and I drive off.

The puppy is already taking over. He's on my knee, sniffing my hands, having an experimental chew at the strap of my shoulder bag. 'He's part Alsatian, I know that,' Sonny says. 'And probably a mixture of three or four others too. Who knows.'

I have more questions for Sonny but at the moment I'm content to be distracted by the little dog. 'I'll have to get him some dog food, and biscuits, and toys. Lots of things.'

'I've got some things for him in the back,' Sonny says. 'I thought we'd go to the house first, check that the power's up and running. Then I can take you to the shops, if you like. You're probably going to need a car or something, living out here. I could leave you this one for a while till you see how you go. It's not that flash, I know. But it's better than the old fishing van.' He laughs.

'Sonny, I haven't got a driver's licence. I mean I can drive, but . . .' I leave it at that, choosing not to tell him about destroying all of Ruby Summerton's identifying documents.

'Oh, well, you can get one issued here when you get around to it. In the meantime, what about a pushbike? Can you ride a bike?'

'I suppose so. I mean I've never tried, but it can't be that hard, can it?'

'You've never ridden a bike?' He sounds incredulous. Never ridden a bike, never owned a puppy. I suppose he's thinking what a strange life. I'm not even sure how to go about planting this flowering creeper.

We're at the house. I carry the puppy up the path, then put him down when Sonny hands me the key. Out of the corner of my eye I see someone sitting on the bench under the apple tree. 'Good heavens,' Sonny says. 'It's Mum.' He goes over to her. 'Hi, Mum, how on earth did you get here?'

She ignores him, her eyes behind the round glasses fixed on me. I start to shake, remembering vividly the shock of the encounter with her yesterday.

'I've brought some things for Miranda,' she says.

Sonny picks up the plastic bags that are lying at her feet. She waits while I unlock the door and then ask her to come in.

She's brought tea and milk and biscuits and tomatoes and butter and bread and Vegemite and a can of dog food. Sonny puts them on the kitchen table which still gleams from yesterday's dusting.

She sits down, her eyes still on me. 'Now we can have a cup of tea,' she says, and chuckles.

'Hang about, Mum,' Sonny says. 'We don't know if Miranda's got power yet, let alone running water.'

He turns on the cold tap. Nothing happens, then there's a whine and a great gush of brown water comes from the tap. The water starts to clear after a few seconds. 'Looks okay,' he says. He tries the light switch. The bulb in the ornate Victorian fitting above the table lights up, then flickers and dies. 'Bulb's blown. But at least there's power so you'll be safe to boil the jug. I'm bringing a sparky mate around tonight when he finishes work to check all the wiring for you.

Just in case there's been a rat or two having a chew over the years.'

At the word 'rat' the puppy stops eating my shoe-laces and growls. 'He'll keep the rats away,' I say, bending to scratch his ear. I'm feeling incredibly happy.

'Can't you find something to see to outside?' Mum Manuatu says to Sonny.

'Yeah,' he says, grinning. 'I'll see if Magda's old push-bike's still in the shed. It'll do for Miranda, maybe.'

Mum Manuatu watches him go, then leans forward toward me. 'Good job. That's got him out of the way. I've got something for you.'

Across the table she pushes a flat oblong package. It's neatly wrapped in white paper. My fingers tremble as I ease off the sticky tape. I can tell already it's a framed picture – a photograph. It's a photograph of Magda, her head and shoulders. She's laughing, her eyes focused straight at the camera lens. Her long straight hair is parted in the middle and tucked behind her ear on one side. She's wearing a circle of small white flowers around her forehead, a white dress with a square neck. It's as if she's sprung to life, just for an instant.

'A wedding-day picture,' Mum Manuatu says. 'I think you should have it.'

'You're being very kind to me.'

'I wasn't yesterday.'

'It's forgotten.'

I tell her – because suddenly she's very easy to talk to – about losing the only photo I had of Magda all those years ago, and then about finding the other photos, the undertaker's photos, at Gran's.

'Sonny told me she drowned. It's hard to believe she ended like that. Sonny was upset last night. Stayed up very late on the beach.'

'I realised I must have been a shock to him, springing out of the blue – '

'Don't worry. He's pleased you're here.'

'Why did she run away? It can't have been just because I wasn't Sonny's daughter.'

Mum Manuatu shrugged slightly, sighed. 'She was a very troubled girl in those last few months. She was surrounded by death. You could see it growing day by day in her eyes. As if she couldn't turn around but another loved one would be lost. In a few months her grandfolks went, and little Ruby, and Sonny was away fighting and for a long time he was listed as missing. When you were born you were sickly, always crying. She wouldn't let you out of her sight.'

'She told people I was Ruby.'

'Perhaps it was a way of tricking the bad spirits snapping at her heels.'

There's an old electric kettle on the end of the bench. It's criss-crossed inside with cobwebs and crusted with dried water salts. I rinse it with cold water from the tap. Mum Manuatu is quiet, perhaps sensing I need a few moments to think. I fill the kettle and plug it in, waiting until the movement in the water tells me the element is working. 'If it was bad spirits she was running away from, they caught up with her. You know, all the time I was growing up, from as long as

I can remember, I had someone talking to me inside my head. She was very real. I've always known her as Miranda. She wasn't always friendly.'

I see Mum Manuatu's eyes move sideways fractionally, as if to check no one else is in the room. 'Some would say that the little dead one was jealous of you. You had life, and you had Magda all to yourself, and you even had the dead one's name. But that's hocus-pocus. Most likely you were lonely, missing your mother. You had the voice to keep you company.'

Sonny's in the kitchen with us. He rinses his hands under the tap and takes over the tea-making. 'Nothing wrong with that bike that a bit of oil won't fix. You can try it out when I come back with the sparky tonight, Miranda.'

He's broken the eeriness that was building up. Mum Manuatu's last sentences were sensible, matter-of-fact, and that was all he had heard.

'I'll bring the rest of your things in, Miranda, and then, Mum, when we've had this cup of tea, we'll go and let Miranda get settled.'

It takes longer than the afternoon to settle in. Sometimes over the next few days I feel as if I'm play-acting, living in someone else's life. It's having all these rooms to wander from one to the other, and drawers and cupboards of possessions which aren't mine. But I'm learning to fit in. Every day it seems more natural to be here. I don't want to be anywhere else.

I kept the puppy, of course, and I call him Jupiter. He never lets me out of his sight. He eats like a horse.

It's good that he likes fish; Sonny brings me more fish than I can eat on my own.

More pieces are fitting into the jigsaw. Mum Manuatu has told me more fragments. It seems Magda shifted back to this house shortly after I was born. Her grandparents had been killed in a car accident at New Year, the start of 1968, the year I was born. So Magda was the last person to live here before I came. And, of course, I spent my first months of life here.

It's strange to look at the folded towels in the linen cupboard and know they were folded by Magda's hands. Then there are her clothes, bright coloured Indian cotton skirts and dresses, embroidered shirts. And all the photos. There are two shoe boxes full, mainly black and white.

There are six or seven wedding-day photos: Magda in the long white dress with the square neck, Sonny looking young and clean-cut and handsome in an obvious army short-back-and-sides. There are other photos of Sonny in his pre-army days with his hair as long as it is now but then jet black. There's a couple in their seventies who I know will be Magda's grandparents – my great grandparents – and I scan their faces carefully, looking for resemblances.

The second shoe box is filled with swimming photos – Magda getting trophies, clippings from newspapers about her, photos of Magda emerging from pools sparkling with water, looking how Sonny first described her to me. These photos and clippings have been carefully kept in date order, as if they were ready to be pasted into a book. The top clipping, the most impressive, is from the Auckland *Herald* in 1966. It's about her swimming scholarship; the headline: 'Medal Prospect from Waihi'. The conviction is growing in me that Magda did not easily throw in her hopes to be a swimming champion. It had been very important to her. Her trophies are tarnished now but they are arranged on a prominent shelf in the sitting room. Married at eighteen with a year-old baby must have been a long distance from representing her country as a swimmer.

In the drawer of the desk where I'm spending hours writing, thinking, dreaming, I find a writing pad and some bills and other papers, and I'm fairly sure that stuffing these things into this drawer and closing it would have been one of the last things Magda did in this house. There's an electricity bill dated September 1968 with a note on it in what I now know is Madga's handwriting: 'Paid. Final reading and power cut off 2 October'. There's a doctor's receipt for a visit on 27 September. There's a loose page in the writing pad with the draft of a letter, perhaps, written on it with many crossings out and corrections, sentences tried out several ways. It could be the draft of the letter that Mum Manuatu said Magda had sent her before she left. This page had in one place 'I'm going to stay with friends down south for a few months. Could you and Sonny when he gets back keep an eye on the house?' Something was crossed out heavily, then: 'Ruby and I won't be back. Sonny can do what he wants to with the house.' 'Ruby' was crossed out and 'Miranda' scribbled above it. Already, then, she was calling me

Ruby; but she couldn't do so in a letter to Mum Manuatu. At the top of the page was the date, 28 September, as if she'd started out to make a fair copy then realised she needed to work out what she wanted to say.

The date is one day after her visit to the doctor, a local doctor. I wonder if he's still in practice here, and if he'd still have records that far back. Or if he'd tell me what was on them if he did. But I feel sure that was the day she found out about her heart condition. That could have been the final thing which tipped her into the madness of disappearing.

Perhaps, for a short time in Australia, she achieved what I suspect she had set out to do. She'd found another family, a secure relationship, a new identity. As Mum Manuatu suggested, she'd cheated the bad spirits snarling at her heels.

There are still some gaps in the jigsaw. Mum Manuatu will eventually fill some of the gaps for me, I think. I haven't found out who Magda's own parents were, or what happened to them. I wonder, too, what it was in the letter that Magda finally sent to Mum Manuatu that made her accept Magda's disappearance so that neither she nor Sonny reported it to the police or tried to find her. But it's a question I can't ask Mum Manuatu, not yet. Perhaps there was bad feeling between them after I was born, and that was why Magda shifted back to this house. Where did she spend the five or six months between leaving here and meeting Rob near Melbourne? And, of course, there's the big gap, one I don't feel ready to wonder about yet, of who was my real father.

I'm recognising the near insanity of Magda's act of disappearance, and I'm starting to worry about my own disappearance. I still feel that Rob discarded me very easily, but I know Gran wouldn't have. She will be worried about me by now. At least Magda had been cool enough to write a letter to cover her immediate tracks; she'd been organised enough even to arrange for the electricity to be cut off.

I write a letter to Gran on Magda's writing pad, telling her I'm all right, and wobble into town on my bike to the post office.

# CHAPTER 19

Today's my nineteenth birthday. Nobody here knows that, except possibly Mum Manuatu.

Sonny threw a party a week ago. He said there was no special reason; the tides had been good and everyone had plenty of fish. In the late afternoon at low tide Sonny and I took the pick-up far along the beach past Bowentown collecting driftwood. On the second trip I drove. There's nothing like careering along hard wet sand. After three trips we had enough wood to build a huge beach fire. It was a still evening. The sun was leaving a cloudless sky. Sonny lit one side of the fire. He said it would burn first and leave embers for cooking.

In the twilight people started to arrive. There were two families with children who ran down the beach and whooped through the shallows of the incoming tide while the adults rolled out mats and blankets and settled themselves near the fire. There were some old people and a group of people about my age. As it grew darker more arrived with drinks and food ready to

174

cook on the fire. Sonny and Mum told me who they were. They all seemed to know who I was, except one old man who had to be helped from the track to the fireside. 'Thank you, Magda,' he said, patting the arm I'd linked through his to steady him across the soft yielding sand.

At first I felt awkward with these strangers. I stuck close to Sonny and his mother, helped watch the shellfish – pipi and mussels – spring open on the tin trays in the heat from the embers, tried to avoid the scalding liquid that ran from them as I flicked them onto paper plates. Someone gave me some insect repellent to rub on against the biting sandflies that hung around my ankles but hardly anyone else's, and the chemical tang reminded me of evenings in Darwin, and Rob. I shut those thoughts out.

There was the sound of guitars tuning in the sandhills beyond the fire. There's no point in thinking of Rob here, or of any of that life.

I was sharing a blanket with a cousin of Sonny's called Shonna who'd been feeding her baby. Now, full and content, the baby boy's eyelids were drooping. 'Would you like to hold him while I get a feed?' Shonna asked me. 'All right,' she went on to the sleepy baby, 'here we are, go to your Auntie Miranda.' I cradled the baby, wrapping the edge of my cloak around him because the coldness of the night was creeping in against the dwindling fire. I thought about Rob's story of my mother cradling me beside a beach fire the first night he met her. I watched how the glow from the fire threw a sheen on the soft brown cheeks of the sleeping baby. I noticed Sonny and his mother looking at me from the other side of the embers. Their faces were full of meaning as if they were seeing Magda sitting with Ruby.

Tomorrow, the day after my birthday, I'm going to see the local historian, the one who wrote the newspaper article about this house. He knows a lot more about Magda's family – my family – right back to Emma Blake herself: my great-great-great grandmother (I think), the woman who first owned this house of mine. I've found more old photos here, many of them yellowed and crumbling with gnawed edges; but some might make sense to him, and he might be able to help match them with names on a family tree I found here, one Magda must have been working on. The later photos – Magda growing up, at school, winning swimming trophies – I've kept separate.

The historian's grandson, the one from the courthouse I met the first day I was here, set up the meeting. His name's Don. Any day now he's going to ask me out, I just know it. Oh, well, I'll probably go. Why not? I remember Kate's advice in the pub near that motel ('loosen up, Ruby'). I was single-minded and over-touchy back then and must have been terrible company. But I'm not Ruby now. I joined the public library here last week and the name on my card is Miranda Brady. It's intoxicating, this shuffle of names to find the one that's right.

I can hear a car. It's turning around on the road outside, stopping at the group of pines in front of the path to the house. It's a new purring kind of car, definitely not Sonny's pick-up. Jupiter hears it too and makes excited runs at the door, wanting to be let out to tear the stranger to pieces. I still freeze at unexpected arrivals. This house, the garden, the trees – they all seem too good to be true. I'm afraid they'll be taken away from me.

I can see the path from where I'm sitting and writing. A man is picking his way carefully over the treacherously rocking paving stones. He's coming to the door. It's Rob.

We don't say anything, just hug for minutes on end. I blot my tears on the slick tailored shoulder of his charcoal suede jacket. After a moment he draws back, still holding my shoulders. 'I could kill you,' he says. 'Disappearing. How could you?'

'How could you marry that dreck Evie?' I answer immediately. I close my eyes, not breathing. That's not what I want to say to him. But then I've nothing planned to say. I didn't expect to be seeing him.

'Ruby. Is that why you ran away?'

'I'm not Ruby now. I'm Miranda.'

He drops his hands, puts them in his pockets and turns away to look through the window. I push the door shut and try to calm Jupiter. Everything's going wrong.

'Would you like coffee? Fruit juice?'

'Look, I didn't drop in for a cup of coffee.'

His back's still towards me. 'Well, I didn't run away, as you put it. You know why I came to New Zealand. It was just when I heard you were getting married I decided it was time to leave you to it. Get out of your way. Make my own way.'

'You didn't consider letting me know about this decision?'

'I didn't think you'd be interested.'

'I didn't know if you were alive or dead. I was on the point of getting the whole New Zealand police force mobilised to find you!'

'They wouldn't have found me.'

He sighs. 'I get it. You replayed Emma's game. Changed your name. Became a new person and disappeared.'

'Not Emma. Her name was Magda.'

'Magda – Miranda – for God's sake what's with all these names? What do they matter?'

'They matter,' I murmur but my words are lost as he moves a chair and sits down at the table.

'I guess I would like a coffee, if it's still on offer. I've driven straight from Auckland.'

I fill the kettle and fiddle with measuring coffee, glad to avoid the direct tension for a few seconds.

'And I find you here, living this utterly mysterious life, throwing new names at me, totally unmoved about my feelings when I heard you'd disappeared – would you *ever* have got round to dropping a postcard? You can't blame me for being devastated. You disappear like that, well, it makes a mockery of all those years.'

He's talking and talking and I can't keep grip on the good reasons I had for starting a new life. And devastated is a new word for him. He must have picked it up from Evie.

I put cups on the table, the plunger pot of coffee, milk. 'Well, you didn't call the cops. So how did you find me?'

After a few seconds he accepts the change of direction. 'I opened a letter sent to you care of Kate in Darwin. I was getting desperate by that stage. I thought it might have a clue in it, and it did. I caught the first flights available and drove straight here.'

'What letter? Who from?'

'It's a clipping from the local paper here, about something called the Emma Blake house being auctioned.' He reached into his jacket pocket and passed me a piece of newsprint. It's the article by the local historian. Across the bottom there's a handwritten message. 'Dear Ruby, if you ever get back to NZ you might check this place out. Good luck. J P Fraser.' Old Mr Fraser. The country and western fan from the motel. It seems like a hundred years ago.

'He must have got the address from Kate, I suppose. But – oh, well, it doesn't matter now.' Nothing matters now. Rob's here, and the hostility between us is melting. It's so good to see him sitting at my beautiful polished table.

'Pour out that coffee and tell me about Emma.'

'Magda. She was Magda Brady, really. And I don't know everything. There are still some mysteries and I think she'd be the only one who could explain them.' I tell him about Sonny and Mum Manuatu and all they knew about Magda, and about Ruby.

He listens silently as I talk. Finally he says slowly,

'It seems macabre to call her new baby by the name of her dead baby.'

'Yes. But then – perhaps it was a way for her to pretend that the death never happened. Who knows? You see there are still these mysteries. There's a mystery about what happened to Magda's own parents. And as for my real father – ' I shrug. 'No clues at all. So far. Perhaps never.'

We talk some more, finish the coffee. I show him around the house. He seems quiet, thinking, perhaps overwhelmed by this new side of his Emma.

I'm wrong. That's not what's in his thoughts. 'It's a cute house,' he says at last. 'I can take care of the outstanding rates, and then you'll be able to put it on the market. I don't know how property's moving here, but it shouldn't be hard to find a buyer.'

'Rob, what are you *talking* about?'

'Well, you're coming back to Australia with me, aren't you, Ruby-baby? I've finished the Darwin contract, but there's another one coming up – '

'Rob! My name's Miranda.'

He laughs. 'Come on, have a heart. I've always called you Ruby. I can't change now. It's not that important, is it?'

'It's important.'

'I see.'

'For a start, it's the name I was given when I was born.' And for another thing if Rob starts calling me Ruby-baby I'll trail after him again and I'll be back where I was a year ago and I'll have achieved nothing. It's like panic rising.

There's a kind smile on his face as if this is a temporary obsession of mine that he'll continue to indulge. I want to shock him out of his complacency, make him feel something of what I have these last few weeks so he'll realise what it means to me to be here.

'Wait here.' I collect the shoe boxes of photos. On the table in front of him I spread Magda's swimming photos, her press clippings, the article about her scholarship and Olympic hopes. He looks at them silently for a long time.

'She was a swimming champion,' he says at last.

'Yes. Rob, that day at Red Beach, the day Magda died, there was no third person there, was there. There was just you and she, no one else.'

From the look on his face I know I've guessed right. I remember the questions about Emma's drowning that haunted me that night at the motel.

'That day at Red Beach,' he starts. I recall what Sonny said about our memories deceiving us, how minds can distort their own histories. I watch the signs of the struggle in Rob's mind showing on his face. Who can ever know the real truth about the past?

I put my hand on his arm. 'Rob. It doesn't matter now.'

'Yes. It does matter. That day at Red Beach we had an argument. It was about all sorts of things – I don't know exactly, perhaps the mystery was getting to me. Anyway, it finally centred on the fact she didn't want to marry me. I didn't stop to find out why. I raced into the sea in a stupid fury and swam out. She brought the board out to rescue me from the rip. It was me she saved. It was my fault she died.'

'It was her heart condition, Rob. It could have happened at any time.'

He doesn't hear me.

'She might have been on the point of telling me everything then. I heard her calling after me that I should wait, she wanted to talk to me.' He spreads his hands flat on the table. 'There. That's what happened. I've never been able to admit it before.'

I go round the table, take his arm, making him stand up. 'Come and look at my garden.'

There's a light wind waving the pinetrees along the edge of the road. The air smells sweet. We wander across the grass in silence. He's recovering his composure.

'I'm sorry,' he says as we go back inside. 'That was not a nice story for you to hear on your birthday.'

'You remembered.'

'When have I ever missed a birthday of yours?' He kisses me on both cheeks. 'Happy birthday. Happy birthday – Miranda. I'll try to call you by your proper name. It's strange that you were Miranda all along. You were your own *doppelgänger*.'

'Gran said that Magda first used the name for my – my invisible companion or whatever you can call it. I suppose it just grew from then. The Miranda person became a strong part of my life. I was still hearing her voice until quite recently.' Or so I think. Our minds distort our own pasts. Suddenly I remember Gran. 'Oh, Rob, how's Gran? Did she get my letter?'

'Not the last time I spoke to her. I'm glad to hear you've written to her, at least. She was upset about this disappearing act of yours.' By now Gran will have my letter, I know, and I'm fairly sure she will understand. I hope she does. Rob's continuing. 'She asked me to give you a message. She finally tracked down Emma's old cloak.'

'She *what*?'

'Emma's – I mean, Magda's, cloak. She found it. In the attic of their old house. It looks pretty tatty. The family which bought the house used the attic as a playroom and all the old clothes for dressing up.'

'You've – you've actually seen it?'

'Oh, yes. She said she'd keep it for you – shall I get her to post it?'

'I – I don't know.' My voice is husky. I'd been *so* sure – 'Rob, I thought I'd found her cloak. I thought I owned the real cloak.'

'Well, so did I. You did, near enough. I told you, it's a classic design.'

All the same, I'd *wanted* it to be my mother's cloak. The identical one. I'd wanted it so much that I'd summoned up Miranda to confirm it for me, and believed in her words all over again.

Rob can see I'm confused, upset. 'Why don't you ring Gran now?' he suggests gently.

I smile at him, trying to shake off this strange sadness. 'The last time I phoned her the line was so bad we ended up misunderstanding each other. Anyway, I haven't got a phone here.'

'No phone? You'll have to get one installed. You can't live here without a phone.'

So. He accepts I'll be staying here. 'I can't afford a phone. And you're not paying for one for me, either. I owe you heaps of money already.'

'I know. I've seen the credit-card statements. Well, I don't know, perhaps I could get a contract around here somewhere and you could work off the debt. And provide me with free board.' Perhaps he sees a flicker of doubt on my face. 'Not a good idea, Miranda?'

He's crafty, dropping the name in like that. But I've got another move. 'What about the wedding, Rob? Remember – Evie?'

'Well. Yes.' He looks at the floor and shuffles fractionally. 'I got a bit distracted from that. I had this missing daughter to worry about.'

'Don't try and make me feel guilty, you rat. You've run out on her, haven't you?'

'It wouldn't have worked, would it?' I get the full blast of those blue eyes, full of innocent appeal. 'Well, what's so funny?'

'It's just that I've – I've heard it all before.'

'It's not that funny. There's no call to laugh that much.' He's laughing too. Then he goes on, lightly, 'And, anyway, you know that I've never found another Emma.'

I nod. It's what he believes. But a small voice from a corner of my head wonders if it's merely a romantic dream of his, an ideal love for ever lost to him. If she hadn't died, how long would they have stayed together? But then perhaps Emma/Magda was extraordinary. She's left a strong image with everyone who knew her, but the images are all in different shades, flickering, changing, and I wonder if I'll ever be able to distil the essential Magda.

Before, at times like this, I might have asked Miranda about it. But I'm on my own now.

# MORE TEENAGE FICTION FROM PENGUIN

☆☆☆☆☆☆☆☆☆☆☆☆☆☆☆☆☆☆☆☆☆☆☆☆☆☆☆☆☆☆☆

### The Lake at the End of the World   Caroline Macdonald

It is 2025 and the world has been cleared of all life by a chemical disaster. But then Diana meets Hector ...

*Winner of the 1989 Alan Marshall Award, named an Honour Book in the 1989 Australian Children's Book of the Year Awards and shortlisted for the NSW Premier's Award. Runner-up for the 1990* Guardian *Children's Fiction Award.*


### Visitors   Caroline Macdonald

Terry's life is filled with so many luxuries that all he really enjoys doing is watching television. One winter's day he realises he isn't alone, someone is trying to get his attention ...

*Winner of the 1985 New Zealand Children's Book of the Year Award.*


### Beyond the Labyrinth   Gillian Rubinstein

Brenton takes his chances in a game which dangerously shadows real life, but who knows where the dice will lead him?

*Winner of the 1989 Australian Children's Book of the Year Award for older readers. Winner of the 1990 SA Festival Award. Shortlisted for the 1989 Alan Marshall Award.*


### You Take the High Road   Mary K. Pershall

When the world suddenly turns dark for Sam and her family, she must struggle to make sense of life's most difficult questions.

*Shortlisted for the 1989 Australian Children's Book of the Year Award.*